## Fairly Certain

"Blimey, 'e's not one of us, is 'e?"

"Nay, not one of us. Look at 'is clothes."

"Is 'e dead?" The British-accented voices murmuring from above began to register, but the snuffling wet nose by Petir's ear drew his immediate attention.

A groan escaped him in response to what felt like a toe nudging him none too gently in his aching ribs.

"Hah! I told you 'e wasn't dead!" cried a voice as the offending toe was removed.

*I guess I fell asleep after all.* He opened his eyes just a slit, grimacing through the glare of early morning sunlight. Confused, he slammed them shut.

*What the hell?* Elves? Or at least a bunch of kids dressed like elves. British elves from the sound of them. He peeked again, then scrunched his eyes closed. And a three-legged dog.

The wet snuffling resumed near his other ear. Petir swatted at the offending beast. A myriad of aches and pains identified his injuries, each vying for his attention. He dropped his elbow across his face with another groan.

"Sit, Trio!" someone commanded. The enthusiastic snuffling ceased.

*A three-legged dog named Trio?* Even through his pain and confusion, he found that one funny.

Hi There!

The original tale about Robin Hood describes an archer/outlaw who stole from the rich to give to the poor. His band of Merry Men included Little John, Friar Tuck, Will Scarlett, Gilbert Whitehand and of course, Maid Marion. The Sheriff of Nottingham and Guy Gisborne were their sworn enemies. In the background of their adventures, Prince John is trying to take the throne from King Richard, the Lionheart. Many were outlawed simply for siding against the usurper.

In *Fairly Certain,* the names have been changed to protect the innocent, so to speak, flipping the tale of Robin Hood on its ~~butt~~ ear. The archer/outlaw in *Fairly Certain* is Maid Rianne (pronounced ree-ANN), the intended of Lord Gisborne. However, she is distracted by a newcomer, Lord Petir (pronounced "Peter"). In a completely unexpected storyline, nothing is as it appears with this merry romp in the days of old, seen through the eyes of the young.

I wanted to share a couple of nuances that tickle me, but most likely no one else will notice. Did you know the word "toward" is used in the USA, but "towards" is used in Great Britain? For the scenes set in the days of Old England, the latter is used, but the Americans use the former. Also, young shoots of milkweed and fern fiddleheads are edible, but the lichen called British Soldiers is not. You'll know what I mean when you read the book. Like I said, nuances.

I hope you have as much fun reading this story as I had writing it. I am looking forward to hearing your feedback. Please visit my website at www.DeborahAnnDavis.com to learn about the next book in the *Love of Fairs* series, *Fairly Safe*, where Mistaken Identity collides with Secret Identity in a tale about a family in witness protection whose cover has been blown.

Have fun today!
Deborah
@DeborahAnnDavis

The first Tale in the

# Love of Fairs Series

# Fairly Certain

*If it be the anniversary of your birth when you first kiss,*
*that blessed moment over the ancient rune becomes your union of destiny.*

# Deborah Ann Davis

Cover art by Rebecca Davis and Katarina Mizla Copyright © 2014
Edited and Formatted by Kate Richard
Printed by King Printing, Inc.

# Fairly Certain

May the Universe
always smile down
on you!

Deborah Ann Davis

# Dedication

First and foremost, to my remarkable Rebecca, who understands my need to write, and never, ever, ever cuts me any slack when it comes to doing the very best you possibly can.

To my fabulous family, who didn't understand why I wanted to write,
but supported me anyway.

And finally, to my magnificent husband, who unwaveringly has made the life I lead possible.

## Acknowledgements

With thanks to Kate Richards, my excellent editor at Wizards In Publishing, and the first person to read my book who wasn't related to me. Your encouragement renewed my determination to see this through.

Thanks to the wonderful authors at my writing groups, CORW and CAPA. Your comradery warmed my soul the first moment I walked through the door.

Thank you to the vendors at the Connecticut Renaissance Faire who taught me about spinning wool, making dyes, tanning leather, a working the bellows. You keep our history alive by living it.

Special thanks to Michelle Vigue (*The Bunker*) who met me on weekends to write, write, write and write.

# CHAPTER 1: To Climb, or Not to Climb

"What do you mean, you can't go?" Petir Capota stopped stuffing his backpack to stare at his roommate, Chris Dunbar, who leaned against his doorframe. Disappointment bubbled up. "Chris, this is our chance to advance in the rankings."

"I know, I know. But my boss called and asked if I could add a few shifts." Chris shrugged, avoiding Petir's glare as he drifted toward his friend's computer array. "I need the dough, bro." From the top of his head to his raggedy Sketchers, Chris was the picture of remorse. Even his crisp, red buzz-cut drooped. His summer job, a vital financial component for keeping their new apartment, had not panned out as expected. Blowing off this chance to put in some extra hours would be a serious mistake.

"Oh, that's just great. First Jimmy bails; now you." Heaving a sigh, Petir plopped down on his bed. He snatched up his favorite Ping-Pong paddle and swiped the air. Like that would change things. "And get your carcass away from my computers."

Unoffended, Chris stepped away from Petir's pride and joy. "You can always go by yourself, dude."

"I can't go by myself. We're supposed to be a team."

"Dude, no one will know."

Jimmy Montana popped his head in the door. "Yeah, Pete, take one for the team."

"Aww, c'mon, you guys. I thought we were taking a week for ourselves."

Jimmy took his customary seat on the floor and leaned against the bed. Despite his blond surfer look, a gift from parents who both hailed from Northern Italy, he'd never touched anything resembling a surfboard. "Hey, I'm really sorry, but—"

"No worries. I got this, Jimmy." Petir sat up, contrite. "Just go to the funeral. Give your mom our condolences."

"Yeah, our condolences, dude." Chris vigorously bobbed his head.

"I don't know why we're bothering to go." Jimmy frowned. "First of all, I didn't even know I had a great uncle. Second of all, she says he was a jerk. I'd rather be geodashing."

Chris laughed. "Sounds like a bumper sticker." He raised his hands to form an imaginary frame. "I'd rather be geodashing."

"So, Chris, what's *your* story?" Jimmy asked.

"I got to work, dude. As my dad would say," his voice dropped in a time-honored imitation of his father, "work equals money, and money equals rent."

Jimmy snorted. "Everything that comes out of your father sounds like a bumper sticker." Neither the guys' parents nor Petir's grandparents approved of their recent decision to leave the dorms to share an apartment, but the boys had scored an affordable unit in Mansfield within walking distance of the University of Connecticut campus. It was shabby and rundown, but within budget. For three guys on the cusp of nineteen, shabby and rundown were in the eye of the beholder.

Petir and his two childhood-friends-turned-college-roommates had always been as different as different could be. However, when faced with a small boy grieving for his parents, both friends had stuck by Petir at a time when others had drifted to a more comfortable distance. They shared an adoration of computers, gaming, and Ping-Pong, but had developed their own interests. Over the years, their bond of friendship had never been dented.

Petir watched Chris, who stared at a window blind's frayed cord as he whipped it repeatedly around his hand. Jimmy was plowing his fingers through his hair. They were obviously as bummed out as he was by the turn of events. Petir sighed. Yeah, he didn't want to kick them to the curb.

"Fine. No worries." He stuffed a sweatshirt into his bag. "I'll be able to hit more dashpoints by myself anyway." He could always come back early if it turned out to be a bust.

"Great!" Jimmy and Chris fist-bumped.

Petir straightened and eyed his two friends. "And no one touches my computers while I'm gone, right?" Despite their own pretty impressive setups, for some reason, they liked to mess with his when they could get away with it.

"Sure, sure." Jimmy nodded.

"You can count on us," added Chris.

"I mean it, you guys." Petir put his hands on his hips. "Neither of you are to use my stuff. You know what happened the last time."

"That wasn't my fault," they chorused.

"Right. I'm still going to lock my door."

"What if you need us to research something for you?" asked Jimmy.

"Here's an idea. Why don't you use *your* computer?" Petir tossed his bag over his shoulder and ushered them out of his room, locking the door behind him. "Alrighty, then. I'm off."

"If you run into any competition, just tell them you're camping," advised Chris, his usual exuberance returning.

"Seriously?" *What was he thinking?*

"With no tent or sleeping bag?" said Jimmy, pushing his glasses up his nose.

"Whatever, dude. You don't want them to think they have to beat you to the cache. Tell them…I know. Tell them you're a tree inspector."

"Shut up, Chris," Petir and Jimmy chorused their automatic response.

"Hey, why don't you stop by your folks?" Chris smacked his lips. "See if you can get *Abuela* to make us some more goodies."

"Now, *that's* a good idea. Her care packages are good for a week." Jimmy adopted his own imitation of Chris's dad. "More Food Equals More Money."

"Sounds like a plan." Petir shouldered his backpack. No problem. He'd hang with nature for a bit, nail a few geo-caches, raise their team ranking, and tuck away a couple of home-cooked meals. It would be more fun with his friends in tow, but he'd be just fine on his own.

*** 

"Let go of me." Rianne spoke quietly, tightly gripping her irritation as she stared at the hand grasping her arm. Where was the giddy feeling the mere sight of Lord Robert usually invoked? His oh-so-handsome face still held those marvelous gray eyes and perfectly even teeth, but, right now, she wanted to punch that flawless nose. The idea of spending the rest of her life with him was rapidly losing its appeal.

He uncurled his grip from her arm and took a step back. "M'lady." He bowed, his attractive face marred by a sneer. "Or should I say, m'lad?"

She bit down on her rising annoyance. They never argued. They always agreed. So why could he not get past this? "What upsets you most, m'lord? That I am disguised as a lad, or that I side with the oppressed?"

"The oppressed? I beg your pardon. They live the life they have chosen. Please, Maid Rianne, think. How will it appear to the sheriff if I allow you to go off into the forest to live with this band of thieves?"

*Allow me?* Even as her anger escalated, she noticed a slight shift in his stance. She braced herself.

"Be reasonable, my dear. I implore you." The sudden seductive quality of his voice caught her off-guard. "Stay here with me, your beloved." He reached toward her neck to capture a tendril escaped from her cap and entwined it around his fingers, staring at it as he had done many a time. She watched him, bemused, her frustration beginning to dissipate. How odd she would rail against him when he grabbed her arm, but he could so easily hold her prisoner by capturing a mere strand of her hair.

And as it had many a time before, self-doubt began to creep into her resolve. Was she truly being petulant and willful?

"Stay. We shall dine together," he continued, still focused on her hair.

What was the point in fighting? Of course they could reach a compromise. After all, with him, she would be free of worry about from where her next meal would come.

He raised his eyes to hers and stepped closer. Now toe to toe with him, she suppressed the urge to step back.

"We shall dance together this night," he murmured.

Rianne tried to focus on his indulgent voice and ignore the triumphant gleam in his eyes. She tensed as his other hand captured her shoulder in a momentary caress then trailed down her arm.

She did not want to jeopardize the relationship she enjoyed with Lord Robert. He was devoted to her, and she wanted to reciprocate. And she did love dancing.

He angled his mouth toward hers. To her surprise, she was leaning toward him.

"I wonder what else we can think of to do together," he said in a soft, husky timbre before he kissed her.

Lord Robert had chosen her when he could have had any maiden. She was indeed fortunate. She sighed as his mouth claimed hers and awaited the return of even bits of her former giddiness, but to no avail.

Raising his head, he gazed into her eyes again, his expression smug. Confused, she laid her head on his shoulder. Had they truly always agreed on everything, or had she merely acquiesced to please him? Perhaps this disagreement was the cause of the missing giddiness, and it would return when all was well between them, but, wrapped in his familiar embrace, it felt like something had changed for her.

"Enjoy the benefits of our station, here at the tournament, my dear," he murmured against her hair. "Stay with me. I shall buy you a beautiful new dress, and—"

Mirth bubbled up in her. "Lord Robert, I cannot compete in a dress."

He released her and stepped back so quickly she staggered with his absence. Alarm flashed through her at his reddened face. She had never seen such a thunderous expression

"You will not compete," he declared. "Archery is a sport for warriors, not wenches."

"Wenches?" Rianne's spine stiffened.

"Aye, wenches. Why? Does the word displease you? What word would you choose?" He regarded her with disdain. "Tell me, Maid Rianne, do you appear more a lady or a wench?"

Unbidden, her palm swung up to strike him, but he captured her hand with a laugh and shoved it away. Without thinking, she took a step back, stripping her bow from her shoulder as she moved. Sweeping the bow in a wide arc, she caught him behind his legs and upended him. He landed on the ground with an audible thump.

He stared at her from the flat of his back, mouth agape. For a moment, she stared back, her own jaw slack with disbelief at her actions. An odd exhilaration filled her.

"The word I would choose is warrior," she said. "I shall see you at the competition, m'lord." She ran off, disappearing into the crowd before he could stop her, but she could not escape his parting words.

"You are no warrior. You are but a maid in boy's clothing and *nothing more*."

What was left of her mind warred with the thrill of her actions. What if he was correct?

\*\*\*

Petir stopped himself from opening his eyes when he realized there were bits of something on his face. Why was he on his back on the ground instead of in a tree searching for the road? Slowly, the details came. He was disoriented by the smell of disturbed earth and decayed leaves filling his nostrils. Or maybe he, in fact, had dirt in his nose. He hadn't actually moved since he fell out of the tree, so he wasn't quite sure. Correction— he hadn't moved since he'd plummeted-rolled-tumbled-slid-crashed down the hill after falling out of the tree.

He groaned aloud as he gingerly surveyed his battered body for damage.

Despite some newly acquired grit, his teeth were intact.

Head still moved although it pounded.

Toes wiggled.

Ribs ached.

Arms and shoulders worked but were sore.

*Yup, Pete, tree climbing was a seriously stupid idea.* At the time, of course, the idea hadn't seemed stupid. How difficult could it be for a lost computer geek to clamber up a low-limbed tree like he was a little kid, get his bearings, and jump down?

Later, he could scold himself for too many hours behind a computer and not enough hours at the tennis table, but right now, he needed to spit. And wipe this crap off his face so he could open his eyes. He brushed his palms off and slowly propped himself on an elbow.

Everything hurt, but it all seemed to be working. That was a relief. He had no backup plan for being alone in the woods with an injury. He spat out what he hoped was only dirt and ran his tongue over the remaining grit while he wiped around his eyes.

*Gross.*

Good thing Chris and Jimmy weren't there. If they had witnessed his impromptu tree dive, he would never have heard the end of it. He rolled over to spit again.

*Holy—* The sudden pain blazing down the back of his leg took his breath away. Alarm shot through him proportional to its intensity.

*Oh, no.* Groaning again, he managed to sit and began brushing at the dirt and leaves falling out of his hair. He probed his leg to locate the injury as he tried to calm the wave of panic rising inside him. To his relief, he found no cut or gash, and no bleeding. Maybe he had pulled his hamstring or something.

*Whatever.* The pain in his leg was unrelenting. What if it was broken?

He glared at the three-story hill which had just hosted his free fall to its bottom. Most likely, he had collided with every one of those fallen limbs and random rocks littering the hillside. His former perch, a large maple tree branch, nestled in the leaves of years gone by, sporting a rotted center. *Seriously?*

He blinked up at the sky. The beginning orange streaks of sunset only added to his anxiety. It would be getting dark soon. He needed a plan.

He picked debris out of his palms. "Okay, I'm sitting in the middle of the woods. *Lost.*" He gingerly fingered an ache on his cheek that felt like a bruise. "Injured … at sunset … talking to myself. Did I leave anything out?" He inspected a scraped elbow. "Oh, yeah. Who's going to miss me?"

*No one, that's who.*

Somehow he was going to have to find his way out of the woods. Maybe his best hope was to try retracing his steps. That meant getting back to the damn tree.

He eyed the hill as he shook leaves out of his shirt and hair. To climb or not to climb, that was the question. Even if he managed to get up the hill, he would still be lost. He was going to have to break down and call his roommates.

*Oh…right.* His cell phone was safely packed away in his backpack.

Which he had prudently hung on another branch of the tree.

Which, of course, had not fallen when he had.

Which was still at the top of the hill.

With no bars.

Petir flopped back into the leaves, his hamstring pain reminding him he had a serious problem. The sky was fiery red on one side and graying on the other. It would be dark *very* soon. Nature was for the birds.

Petir didn't really have a choice. He needed to go for the cell phone and find a location with bars. Ignoring the pain, he sat up and slowly rolled into a kneeling position. *Oww.* Feeling steady, he hauled himself to his feet, favoring his injured leg. *Owww.* Maybe this wasn't going to be so easy. He tried to move forward, but *Owwwww!* The stabbing sensation in his leg from one step told him all he needed to know. There would be no hill climbing today.

"Alrighty, then." He looked around as he tried to calm himself. "It's going to be a warm summer night. Just pretend you're camping." He clumsily lowered himself back down to the ground and began raking the surrounding leaves toward him with his hands. The occasional awkward move made him gasp with pain, but eventually he produced a leafy bed of sorts. He untied his jacket from his waist and lay down. Flapping it in the air, he settled the jacket over his torso like a blanket. Exhausted by the nagging pain, he hunkered down for the night.

*This actually isn't so bad. It's pretty warm, and there're stars out, so at least there won't be rain.* He removed a twig from under his shoulder blades and closed his eyes. *Abuelo always says I can fall asleep anywhere.*

Something crackled in the growing darkness. Eyes flying open, all of him froze except for his revving heart. Wasn't there a story about a bear roaming across the library lawn in Simsbury? But he was near Guilford. He was fairly certain Guilford was pretty far from Simsbury, so he should be safe. Maybe the story wasn't even about a bear.

A branch snapped in the distance.

Nope, the story was definitely about a bear. He sat up in alarm, pain shooting down his leg. Hugging his jacket, he tried to peer through the night.

Nothing.

He strained to hear what his eyes were incapable of revealing. Somewhere on the hill, he detected leaves rustling.

*Oh no.* He concentrated all of his energy on the noise. *Do you run when you see a bear, or do you stay still?*

After a short eternity, he concluded the wind had disturbed the leaves, not a Petir-hunting predator.

"Get a grip! A bear in Connecticut? C'mon," he muttered.

Still listening, he forced himself to lie back down. In the ensuing, cricket-enhanced silence, he resolutely closed his eyes, only to have his attention snap toward rustling in yet another direction. *Connecticut has coyotes. I should've climbed the damn hill.*

No way was he going to sleep.

It was going to be a long night.

## CHAPTER 2: What the Hell?

"Blimey, 'e's not one of us, is 'e?"

"Nay, not one of us. Look at 'is clothes."

"Is 'e dead?" The British-accented voices murmuring from above began to register, but the snuffling wet nose by Petir's ear drew his immediate attention.

A groan escaped him in response to what felt like a toe nudging him none too gently in his aching ribs.

"Hah! I told you 'e wasn't dead!" cried a voice as the offending toe was removed.

*I guess I fell asleep after all.* He opened his eyes just a slit, grimacing through the glare of early morning sunlight. Confused, he slammed them shut.

*What the hell?* Elves? Or at least a bunch of kids dressed like elves. British elves from the sound of them. He peeked again, then scrunched his eyes closed. And a three-legged dog.

*Get a grip, Petir!*

The wet snuffling resumed near his other ear. Petir swatted at the offending beast. A myriad of aches and pains identified his injuries, each vying for his attention. He dropped his elbow across his face with another groan.

"Sit, Trio!" someone commanded.

The enthusiastic snuffling ceased.

*A three-legged dog named Trio?* Petir snorted. Even through his pain and confusion, he found that one funny.

"I shall fetch the 'ealer!" said a young voice.

*Eeler? What the hell is an eeler?* Listening to the departing footfalls reminded Petir he was lying on the ground in a forest. A feeling of unease filled him. *Okay, maybe I haven't actually woken up yet. This could just be some stupid dream.*

Warm air wafting across his face replaced the cold, moist nose in his ear. He stole another look to find a boy on his haunches, scrutinizing him. Topped by a jaunty hat, a fringe of red hair bordered his freckled face. A halo of treetops framed his head. His slightly grubby countenance broke into a delighted smile as he patted Petir on his bruised arm.

"Pray be at your ease, m'lord. The 'ealer will have you right as rain in no time."

A ring of curious boys' heads popped into view, obscuring the treetops. Petir made them disappear by closing his eyes. *M'lord? Really polite British elves. In Connecticut? I don't think we're in Guilford anymore, Toto.*

Jeez, he was sore. It felt like he had received a good beating. He hadn't been this sore when he lay down.

Must be a stress dream.

Petir began to test his limits, starting with his knees His stiffened ribcage and back ached with every move. And what the hell was going on with his leg? The back of his left thigh throbbed like crazy. He didn't remember feeling such extreme pain in a dream before. Head pounding, Petir rolled to his side. Several feet scrambled away from him.

"Take heed! 'E's moving!" cried one of the children.

Surprised, Petir paused, propping himself on his elbow.

"Hey, calm down!" he grunted. "I'm not going to hurt you." The grungy group eyed him from several yards away. He counted half a dozen boys, ranging from about nine to seventeen years old. They wore loose-fitting green or brown tunics over baggy cut-off pants. Most sported some type of cap on their heads.

*What's with all the mini Peter Pans?* Definitely a dream.

One of those weird dreams.

Petir pushed himself into a sitting position, groaning as he went. The redhead started forward as if to help, but an older boy restrained him.

"Eh, now, Cord!" the older boy snapped. "Stay back! It could be a trap!"

"A trap?" said the smaller boy derisively. "Look at 'im, Dale. 'E's hurt!"

"A trap?" echoed Petir. *Paranoid mini Peter Pans.* "A trap? Jeez! What kind of idiot would set a trap in the middle of the woods?"

"The type of idiot who knows where young boys like to play," replied a cold female voice behind him.

## Chapter 3: Maid Rianne

Her stance was relaxed, her feet about a shoulder's width apart. Backlit by the sun peeking through the trees, the loose leggings she wore hinted at the shape of her legs. The shapeless jacket topping them was cinched at a small waist. A bow was draped over her shoulder, and an accompanying quiver of arrows hung across her back, its sling defining curves hidden by the baggy jacket. One hand rested on a sheathed dagger hanging from the belt. In the other, she held what looked like a walking stick. She stood there, a true warrior, her sharp gaze appraising the scene, ignoring the tail-wagging, three legged dog competing for her attention.

*Wow! What movie did she just walk out of?* As far as he knew, girls from Connecticut didn't walk around armed to the teeth. Unexpectedly, this dream had just developed some serious potential.

As she stepped closer, the sunlight splashed across her face, revealing a scowl. Her black-brown hair was all but hidden under a peaked green cap. Her gaze narrowed at his open-mouthed stare. He snapped his jaw shut and began scrambling to his feet. He barely registered the boys skirting him to stand by the warrior girl. Most of his attention was hijacked by his thigh. Shocked by the sudden onslaught of pain, he collapsed on the ground, gasping as he grabbed his leg.

Could there be this kind of agony in a dream?

"Take this, John." The girl shoved her walking stick at one of the larger boys.

"But, mistress," he protested as she handed the bow to another boy, "if 'tis indeed a trap?"

*Mistress?* Petir eased himself into a sitting position, trying to decide if he dared massage his injury.

"With you wielding the staff and Dale the bow, I shall be well protected." She smiled reassuringly at the boy as she unslung the quiver and passed it to the one called Dale.

John followed her back to Petir, slapping the staff against his palm. Dale hastily notched an arrow into the string and aimed it at Petir's chest.

"Hey, watch where you're pointing that thing!" cried Petir, extending his arm as if it could ward off an arrow.

"Behave, m'lord, and no harm will befall thee." John's grim tone matched his expression.

The girl dropped to her knees by Petir's side. "Where are you hurt, m'lord?" she asked, her manner brusque, but her fingers gentle as they inspected his battered cheek.

*Oww.* He pulled his face away from her fingers.

"I ... I'm not sure. Everything hurts." Although he still focused on the cocked bow shaking in the boy's grip, the rest of his attention zeroed in on her and her fresh outdoor fragrance. *Nice.*

"Were you in a fight?" She ran practiced fingers over his arm, her head lowered as she focused on her task.

Petir stopped breathing and stared at her blankly. This was different. In the last two years, the only females who ever touched him were related to him. Or cleaning his teeth. They certainly weren't cute girls dressed up like a female Robin Hood.

A few rebellious curls escaping from her hat outlined the curve of her cheek. Oh yeah. She was cute, but it was her confidence and grace that cranked her up to *hot.* Even though it hurt when she touched him, the simple act of running her fingers along his arm was reducing him to stupid, leaving him with all the capabilities of a puddle, including a puddle's ability to hold a conversation. He had nothing to say. Absolutely nothing.

What was there to say anyway? *Come here often?*

She shifted to his collar bone. Judging by her behavior, she seemed to have no idea how her touch affected him outside of the pain she was evoking. He was fairly certain it was fortunate she was causing him to wince; otherwise, he might be embarrassing himself in front of all these kids.

"M'lord? Were you in a fight?" she repeated, this time louder and slower as if talking to an simpleton. Her prodding fingers moved to his ribs as he grimaced.

*Yeah. You should see what I did to the other guy.* "No," he managed to mutter. He didn't want to appear to be an actual idiot, but… "I fell out of a tree."

"Pardon, m'lord? I did not hear you."

"I fell out of a tree, okay?" Petir's face heated.

A moment of silence greeted his confession, followed by a burst of laughter from the boys. The girl by his side ducked her head to hide a grin.

Irritated, he snapped, "And who are you supposed to be? Robin Hood and her Merry Men?"

With the boys snickering behind her, she chuckled as she reached across his body to examine the other side. "Not likely! You may address me as Maid Rianne. And your name, sir?"

"Petir. Petir Capota."

"Ah, as in Saint Peter, one of the patron saints of travelers. He must be responsible for us coming to your aid."

"Well, I'm P-E-T-I-R, not P-E-T-E-R." Squirming, Petir grabbed Maid Rianne's wrist. "Look, I really appreciate the exam and all, but it's my leg. Okay? My leg needs help."

Startled, her eyes swung toward his, and whoosh! All the air left his lungs.

*Brown eyes.*

*Very brown eyes.*

*Very brown eyes with dark rings around them.*

*Very brown eyes with—*

*Oops.*

Her very brown eyes narrowed. John and Dale took an anxious step closer.

*Uh oh. You think I'm coming on to you.* Petir released her like she was a hot potato. *As if anyone would ever put a computer geek like me and a hottie like you in the same sentence.*

"No, honest." He cocked his palms back in surrender. "I can't stand. Watch!" He rolled to his side and began to repeat his previous night's attempts to get to his feet, but she restrained him.

"That will not be necessary, m'lord." She pressed him back down and assumed a position closer to his leg. Her skilled fingertips resumed their exploration.

*Whoa! This is way worse.* Computer jockeys might not ever get hot babes checking out their ribs, but they absolutely did not get them feeling up their legs. But here was this babe doing things his leg had only dreamed of.

*Wish I had my cell phone so I could take a selfie. Hey there, Mistress Hottie, would you mind posing for a picture so I can prove you groped my leg?*

Whoops! Her fingers drifted a little too high. *Okay, this could end up being embarrassing.* He needed a distraction, and he needed it fast.

*Conversation. Yeah, that's the ticket.*

"Hey, you, uh, really know what you're doing. Are you some kind of—" His attempt to chat her up ended in a yelp as she probed the site of his injury.

Maid Rianne sat back on her heels, hands at her waist, as Petir gingerly rubbed the back of his leg. She pondered the situation, her teeth tugging at her lower lip.

*Females biting their lips is definitely underrated.*

Sighing, she looked over her shoulder and addressed the boys. "We cannot leave him here to fend for himself. We shall have to drag him."

*Drag me?*

"Fetch at least two large branches. We can lash smaller branches to them with vines."

"But, m'lady, we canna bring him back to the camp! He might be a spy!" Dale's brow furrowed as he shook brown hair out of his eyes, still pointing the bow at Petir.

*A spy? In Connecticut? Whatever for?*

"He could lead them right to us," said a frizzy-headed blond boy with a scowl.

*Lead who?*

Maid Rianne faced the boys. "As to his fate, 'tis not our decision to make. We shall bring him back to the camp blindfolded and let the elders decide. Off with you." She tilted her head toward the trees.

After a moment's hesitation, Dale lowered the bow, nodded to John, and turned toward the brush. Immediately the others scampered off in different directions, leaving John smacking the walking stick in his palm. Maid Rianne held out her hand, and John reluctantly returned the staff to her. She nodded as if to reassure him, but instead of following the others, John retreated to a nearby tree and squatted against it. From there, he seemed content to glower at Petir.

Petir cleared his throat. "I guess he kind of has a crush on you, huh?" He nodded toward her protector.

"A crush, m'lord?" Maid Rianne frowned.

"You know, he ... you know ... he likes you," Petir floundered as she looked at him. He was fairly certain they didn't use the word "crush" where she came from.

"Likes me, m'lord?" Maid Rianne furrowed her brow. "We side together for the same cause, our fight against oppression from tyrannical rulers. He merely stays to protect me should you be revealed a clever trickster."

"Clever trickster? Not me!" Petir raised his palms in a defensive gesture. "I'm not at all clever. I mean, I'm clever, but I'm no trickster."

She quirked a delicate brow.

*Great eyebrows.*

"Oh, really, m'lord?"

Heat rose around his neck as she studied him.

"And how is it that you come to be in these woods, with your foreign talk, and your odd clothing?" she asked.

"*My* foreign talk? *My* odd clothing?" Petir sputtered "What about you and the seven dwarves?"

"Seven—?" She leaned back on her haunches, hands on her hips. "You would insult those who would come to your aid, sir? Perhaps we should simply be off and let the soldiers help you find your way."

"Oh, the soldiers, huh?" His voice dripped sarcasm. "You mean the ones who work for the tyrannical rulers and cause all the oppression?" Sarcasm, it turned out, helped keep the rest of him in check. "Look, I'm more than sore, and I appreciate playing bows and arrows as much as the next guy, but—"

"Playing bows and arrows?" the girl parroted, irritation sweeping her face.

"Well, yeah. You know, a girl like you, armed to the teeth—"

"A girl like me?"

She sprang to her feet, twirling the staff faster than he could follow. Her spinning staff traced an arc over her head then slammed into the ground, inches from Petir's ear. Only the floating leaves landing on his scrunched-closed eyes disturbed the silence. Petir carefully opened his eyes, ignoring the fresh aches created by his manly cringing.

She straightened gracefully after her lunge and rested the staff on her shoulder.

"A girl like me, m'lord?" She spun on her heel and walked away.

John smirked from his position by the tree.

"Whoa!" breathed Petir. He propped himself on his bruised elbows and surveyed the dent in the ground left by the staff. *What the hell?* That could have been his head.

*Maid Rianne? Ha! More like Mad Rianne. Or Maid Xena, the Warrior Princess.*

The boys trickled back with bundles of branches. John stood and brushed himself off. "I wouldna make her angry, m'lord," he threw over his shoulder in Petir's general direction.

"You think?" Petir lay back down, grunting as another stab of pain shot down his leg. Maybe he needed to rethink the whole dream thing and figure out what was happening to him. He needed more info. He targeted the smallest boy who was assembling branches.

"So, what's going on here? A camping trip? Some kind of club?"

The boy paused at Petir's words. "Club, sir? Nay, I have no club. I have a quarterstaff back home, but carrying a weapon is not permitted for the young."

"Oh, of course not. No weapons for the young. Right. Makes sense." *A quarterstaff? Is that a real word?* "Hey!" Petir propped himself up again, ignoring his aches. "Can you get my cell for me? It's in a tree. I can just call for help, and you...nice people...can go back to doing whatever it is you were doing."

"We were gathering fiddleheads for dinner," supplied the smallest boy.

*Fiddleheads for dinner? Maybe in Wonderland.*

"A cell?" repeated John, frowning. "In a tree?"

*Right. The Merry Men did swords, not cell phones.*

"Why do you speak in such an odd fashion?" asked the redheaded boy as he laid small branches across two larger ones.

"Ignore his babble," Maid Rianne commanded. She frowned at Petir. "He most likely is addled from a blow to the head."

"Who, me? I'm not addled. This is the way I always talk. What's wrong with it?"

"You do not sound like you belong with us, m'lord." The smallest boy steadied the sticks while the redhead lashed them together with vines. "Methinks you must be from another place entirely."

*And another century entirely.* "*Me* thinks I talk like all the other Connecticut Yanks talk. That's what *me* thinks."

"Connect to cut?" The boy grinned. "Connect what? To cut what?"

Was the kid jerking his chain? Or.... "Okay, I get it. You're tourists, and you don't know where you are. This is Connecticut, and—"

"Nay, your lordship," interrupted Maid Rianne, her expression indiscernible. "This be the king's own forest."

"King? There is no king."

Several of the boys stopped what they were doing to gape at him. The dismay and alarm portrayed in their faces made Petir very uneasy.

"No king?" growled John. "I will not be a party to helping a traitor to our good king."

"We should not help him," the blond boy said. "He does not recognize good King Richard."

If this was a dream, it was turning creepy. Maid Rianne interrupted his thoughts again by walking his way.

*Wow! She even makes walking look good....*

*Wait. What was I saying?*

She leaned over and rested a cool hand on his brow. Petir's mouth went dry.

"Does your head pain thee, m'lord?" she asked, her face troubled.

"A little. I...uh, not much. I mean, it was, but now it...it's...." Maid Rianne squatted next to him and gently ran her fingers through his hair. That had *never* happened to him before.

"Enough talk, m'lord," she instructed. "You should rest."

*Whatever you want, Maid Rianne.* Petir fell silent, enjoying her touch. It was glorious. This was turning out to be an excellent dream. He felt wonderful. He felt bewitched. He felt—

"Yow!" he yelped. "What was *that*?"

"M'lord, you have quite a bump here, but no bleeding. You must have hit your head when you fell."

*Jeez. That really hurt.* He winced as he inspected the site himself.

Maid Rianne put her palms on either side of his face and turned him to look at her. Petir froze. A patch of sunlight beamed down between the trees behind her, creating a halo effect around her face. She moved her head slowly side to side, allowing the sun to splash across his face as she moved. She stared long and searchingly into his eyes. He stopped breathing, his pain unceremoniously shoved to the back seat.

She cleared her throat and released his face. "Your eyes show no ill effects from the blow, m'lord." She held up three fingers. "How many do you see?"

She was only checking his vitals? He almost laughed aloud at his mistaken read of her actions.

*Nice hands.*

"M'lord?"

"Oh! Uh, three."

"All appears well, m'lord, but you should be watched 'til the next dawn."

"Who..." Petir licked his dry lips and tried to swallow in his dry throat. "Who will watch me?"

"The 'ealer, of course, yer lordship," piped up the redheaded boy.

*What the hell is an eeler?*

"Hey, Red, what's your name?" Petir asked.

The kid gave Petir a cheeky grin. "They call me Cord, m'lord."

"Okay, Cord, what's an eeler?"

"Why, a person who tends to wounds and 'eals the sick, sir."

"Okay, wait. Do you mean a *healer*?"

"'Tis what I said, sir."

"Yes, of course," said Maid Rianne, smoothly standing while rubbing her hands on her pants.

*I hope my hair's clean.* Petir touched the lump on his skull as he watched Maid Rianne rejoin the boys. Baggy clothes or not, she was kicking the warrior maiden thing.

A stretcher with a yoke took shape under the boys' industrious hands. Using vines, they secured the smaller branches between two larger limbs. A third ran perpendicular to the first two.

They worked quickly, speaking in hushed tones, occasionally glancing over their shoulders into the forest, as if dreading unwanted company. Petir followed their gazes, wondering what caused their concern. Could it be the soldiers mentioned earlier? Should he be worrying, too?

Eventually they lifted the stretcher and carried it to Petir. It looked uncomfortable and unstable.

"I'm not getting on that."

"Oh, but you are, m'lord." Maid Rianne's voice was calm but firm. "Consider your limited options." She began counting on her hand. "You may get on, be blindfolded, and be carried to our camp. Or," her sarcastic words belied her sweet smile, "you can try to walk to the camp blindfolded, which I do not recommend."

"Or you can find your own way back from whence you came." She paused, solemnly gazing at him over three fingertips. "Tell me, m'lord. Do you know where you are?" She arched her brows at his frown. "I thought not." She folded down one of her fingers with feigned politeness.

"I know where I am. I'm in a damn nightmare," he growled. Hottie or not, she was beginning to piss him off.

"Or, m'lord, you could simply remain here until you heal, then leave on your own accord." The finger reappeared while she pretended to sigh regretfully. "Such a difficult decision is yours."

The boys giggled, not the least bit cowed by Petir's glare.

"Your decision, sir?" Maid Rianne asked, her features schooled into exaggerated patience.

"Fine!" snapped Petir. "I'll ride that thing, but I am *not* wearing a blindfold."

"No blindfold? As you wish, m'lord." Maid Rianne lowered two fingers. "However, that reduces your choices by more than half. Shall you be spending the night here, or making your way back?"

*That was cold.* He looked at the boys, who were now avoiding his gaze. Even John had an air of concern as he frowned at the twig he was holding. The smallest kid was actually wringing his hands while he looked back and forth between Petir and Maid Rianne.

His head resumed its pounding in double time. Perhaps he needed to rethink his stance. After all, if this was a dream, it didn't matter if he went or not. Refusing the blindfold, however, could result in Maid Hottie exiting the dream permanently. That would suck. Unless another hot maiden put in an appearance.

But, what if it wasn't a dream? He still didn't know where he was, and unless some bars magically appeared on his cell phone, he was going to end up sitting on his butt in the woods another night. Not to mention, he didn't know where his cell had gone.

On the other hand, maybe these kids came from some kind of psycho cult and were hiding out. The deranged always acted suspicious in the movies.

"Nope. I'm not wearing the blindfold. I don't know you people. For all I know, you could—"

"Oh, please, sir! Accept the blindfold!" cried the small boy.

Petir blinked, his unease growing. The boy's angst was contagious. Cord touched Maid Rianne's arm. "Please, mistress, we cannot leave him here."

"We can, and we will," she replied, shaking him off. "I, for one, am not willing to betray our cause simply because a stranger refuses a blindfold. Are you?" She leaned forward. "And what if this is nothing more than an elaborate plot to reveal our whereabouts? Men, women, and babes—all sacrificed for a moment of kindness. Your family. Their families...."

The boy's head dropped as he stepped away from her and closer to Petir. "It is not right, mistress. It is just not right," he muttered.

Maid Rianne straightened. "May I suggest you head back to the camp and ask for a volunteer to help bring this stranger to the nearest town? Perchance there be one who is willing to risk capture *and* spending the remainder of his days as a guest of the sheriff. But not I." She strode to Petir. "Your final decision, yer lordship?"

"Please, m'lord." Cord ran over and squatted next to him. "Ye be better off with us. I will not let any harm come to you."

Petir closed his mouth, which had somehow started hanging open again, and regarded the distraught young face. This kid was going to protect him? He probably didn't even reach Petir's shoulder.

*Who are they? And what the hell is going on?*

Good question.

"Who are you guys, and what the hell is going on? Are you in some kind of trouble?"

"Only if we get caught," sneered John.

"Caught? Why? Did you do something wrong?"

"Is feeding your family wrong?" snapped Maid Rianne. "Is avoiding the tax collector when you have no money wrong? Is standing against oppression wrong?"

"I ...no ...except the tax thing. You could work things out with the tax collector."

"Work things out with the tax collector? Have you indeed sided with the sheriff then, m'lord?" Her voice was tense and low.

His would be rescuers drew into an uncertain huddle. The mood had shifted, and it was not a shift in his favor *Okay, this is moving up the creepy scale.*

"Sheriff? Nooo. I definitely have not sided with the sheriff. I don't know any sheriff."

Maid Rianne continued to study Petir distrustfully.

He needed to do something fast. He sure wished his head would stop pounding so he could think.

"M'lord?" entreated Cord.

"Fine!" he spat out. "Help me onto that rickshaw thing, and get me a damn blindfold!" A British psycho cult...hiding from the sheriff...in the woods of Connecticut. This had better be a dream.

Cord's face broke into a wreath of smiles.

"Your chariot awaits, yer lordship." John extended his arm with a flourish. Petir hesitated, then seized the offered forearm. Dale grabbed Petir's other arm. The two boys hoisted him to his feet and eased him onto their contraption.

Foreboding filled Petir as he watched the blindfold head for his face.

*I should never have climbed that damn tree.*

# Chapter 4: Petir Goes to Camp

With more than a few misgivings, Petir began the journey away from a doctor and civilization and deeper into this weird realm, acutely aware that he was at the mercy of these strangely dressed kids with their foreign accents, their random collection of weapons, and their *extremely* uncomfortable stretcher.

As they dragged him across the bumpy forest floor, he attempted to stabilize both his head and leg while gripping the stretcher for balance. What else could this be if it wasn't a dream? Reality? Forget that. Sure, he had never been found sleeping in the forest before, but he was pretty sure that if he had been, his rescuers would have had American accents and T-shirts, not bows and arrows. Nope, definitely not reality.

Maybe he had hit his head harder than he thought when he fell out of the tree. Maybe he was in a coma, and his mind was concocting all this. His anxiety ratcheted up a notch. *That would really suck.*

The dream option was much more appealing. For all he knew, it was still Friday. He would be waking soon and getting ready to go to his summer job—a nice ordinary day at work.

Dropped cell service would not be screwing up a geodash competition late Friday afternoon, eliminating his only GPS guide. He would not be lost in the woods without any bars on his phone, and he would not be climbing a tree like an idiot, trying to relocate the road.

He would be waking up in his own bed, alone, getting ready for work and looking forward to smoking Chris and Jimmy at Ping-Pong. He would not be surrounded by Mad Rianne and the Seven Dwarves with no idea how he got there.

However, for a dream, everything seemed excessively real; his headache, the pain shooting down his leg as the makeshift stretcher bounced around, the smell of the forest air, the noises behind the stretcher, the hungry growl in his stomach. Way too much detail for a dream.

But what else could explain his presence in olden days England?

*I suppose all dreams have this degree of detail, and I forget when I wake up. Just like I'll forget most of this. I might as well go with it. I've steered dreams before.*

He shifted his weight, wishing he could see where they were going. This trip seemed to last forever.

"Hey," he called to no one in particular, "what's that sound behind us?"

The stretcher jerked to an abrupt halt, and all noise ceased around him. Even blindfolded, he could perceive the tension in the group. It was palpable.

"What's the mat—" A hand clamped over his mouth.

"M'lord," Maid Rianne's soft voice breathed in his ear. "Quietly now. What sound?" She removed her hand so he could speak.

Petir aimed his head at her voice to answer, but her breath wafted across his lips, turning him stupid again.

"M'lord?" she pressed.

"Um, right," Petir stammered. "It was kind of like a brushing, no, a raking sound, right behind the stretcher." He felt Maid Rianne expel a breath of relief as she leaned back and chuckled.

"That, m'lord, is the sound of the lads concealing our path with dry leaves." She stood and walked away.

Great! Now no one would find him. Not that anyone would be searching. He said he'd be gone for at least a week. Wait. What was he worried about? This was only a dream, right?

"Mistress." A young voice trudging alongside the stretcher interrupted Petir's thoughts. "Surely there is no harm in removing the blindfold now. We are just outside the encampment."

"Methinks you are correct, m'lad." Maid Rianne spoke from the head of the stretcher. "M'lord, you may remove your blindfold."

Blinking away the glare of unaccustomed light, Petir peered at his surroundings. Lack of a blindfold did not reveal much; only more forest. He could see John standing shoulder to shoulder with Maid Rianne as they dragged him along.

*He's my competition for Maid Rianne.* "How old are you, John?" he asked.

"I have thirteen years, m'lord."

Petir was startled. "Only thirteen?" Easily the largest of the band of merry elves, the kid appeared closer to seventeen. Petir grinned. So much for competition.

"Aye," John acknowledged. "I be big for me age."

"You think?"

A distant shout caused all of them to turn. The boys responded with cheers and waves.

"'Tis about bloody time," muttered one of the stretcher bearers, earning a well-placed cuff to the ear from Maid Rianne.

"Beggin' yer pardon, mistress," he said, rubbing his ear, "but the bloke is bl...— 'e's heavy!"

They lowered Petir to the ground as they waited for a large bearded man to jog down a nearby hill. Laced over a billowy shirt, his vest and pants resembled something from some old pirate movie, right down to the three-cornered hat perched on his head.

"Little John! Wot's this? Wot's this?" he called as he approached. "Someone hurt?"

"Little John?" Petir asked, turning to face the large thirteen-year-old. *Like in* Robin Hood*? I'm having a Robin Hood dream?* Maid Rianne made more sense if this was a Robin Hood dream. Actually, the whole thing made more sense if he was having a Robin Hood dream.

"Nay, sir," giggled the smallest boy. "*I* be Little John because I be the smallest. *He* be Big John. He is big, you see, sir."

"Oh, right. Yeah, I see," muttered Petir. *Okay, wrong story. I guess they're not Robin Hood's Merry Men, or Merry Boys, or whatever. Maybe they're the Lost Boys from Peter Pan.*

Petir groaned aloud. *Oh, please don't let this big hairy guy be Peter Pan! I am not in the mood for a dream that weird.*

"We found him in the forest. He says he fell out of a tree and hurt his leg." Big John gave Petir a skeptical nod.

Maid Rianne approached the newcomer. "He has injured his leg here, and he does have a knot here," she gestured at herself. "But it appears there be no broken bones."

"Here, now, what's your name, young sir?" the man asked as he stroked his beard. Unlike the others, his accent sounded Irish.

"Petir Capota."

"Sir?"

*Oh, right. When in Rome, do what the Romans do.* "Uh, Lord Petir Rojo Capota."

"Ah, Lord Capota. I be Fryer Tuck, and these be me sons, Dale and Little John. How is it you find yourself climbing trees in these woods on this grand day, m'lord?"

"I was, uh, looking for directions." Petir's mind was whirling. Friar Tuck? That sounded Robin Hoodish. *Does Friar Tuck have two sons? Is Little John really supposed to be little?*

"Directions? In the middle of the woods?" queried the burly man.

"He suffers from a blow to the head, Fryer Tuck," reminded Maid Rianne.

"Have ye family or friends who would be wanting news of ye, then?" asked the man, with concern in his blue eyes.

"Nah, I'm on vacation." Petir shook his head. "Some vacation, right?"

Fryer Tuck pursed his lips for a moment as he considered the information, and then gave a short nod. "Ye did right, lass, bringing him here to be seen to. We shall put him in the healer's tent for now."

"Umm, maybe I should go to a doctor instead of spending another night camping," said Petir.

Dale snorted. "*I* shall not be dragging you back through the forest."

Maid Rianne ignored the comment and walked purposefully to Petir's side. Leaning over him, she stared into his eyes. He drew a breath and held it, his brain turning to pudding. She gently brushed his hair from his forehead. His heart began to thump out a beat you could dance to.

*Okay, okay. If she kisses me in front of all these people, I've definitely left reality behind.*

Maid Rianne leaned closer. She raised his eyelid with one finger and peered at him. Disappointment washed over Petir, followed by an inner chuckle. *Apparently, hotties don't kiss geeks in this world either.*

"I see no sign of a problem, m'lord." She released his eyelid and brushed his hair back into place. "I can assure you, m'lord, you will be well-cared for if you decide to stay."

*Whoa. That was a double meaning if I've ever heard one. I'm staying.*

"Fine." He attempted nonchalance despite his delight. "Take me to your leader."

"The elders will meet with you tomorrow, m'lord," said Fryer Tuck. "Your fate will be decided then."

That sounded ominous.

Fryer Tuck signaled the boys, who resumed their positions at the head of the stretcher. Fryer Tuck helped lift it, and they began dragging it up the hill as the younger boys busily covered their tracks. Maid Rianne, however, had paused to remove her hat and shake out her long, dark hair. She rewound her locks and began securing them again under her hat. She tilted her chin, and her eyes met Petir's. Surprisingly, she blushed.

"Maid Rianne, a word please," called Fryer Tuck.

"As you wish, sir." Ignoring Petir, she scooped up her staff and bow and nimbly ran to the head of the stretcher.

Petir sighed as he headed farther into the unknown. Gripping the sides of the stretcher to keep from sliding off, he tried to see the bright side.

*At least I'm going to spend the night in a tent.*

Bump. Bump.

*Ow! And there won't be any wild animals to worry about tonight.*

Bump. Bump. Bump.

*And there're no monsters in this dream.*

Peter adjusted his grip as they headed down the other side of the hill. From there, they followed the notch carved by a stream at the bottom. As they rounded the bend, the sounds abruptly changed. An astonishing sight greeted him

Tucked away in a valley, hidden by three large surrounding hills, nestled a small town of shelters and campfires. Six-foot-tall tents, some of them the size of his bedroom, were made of branches and cloth. All of the men were dressed similarly to his escorts, but the women wore a variety of long skirts topped with blouses. A few dogs and some chickens roamed freely, and a couple of lambs were tethered to a tree. The "townspeople" consisted mostly of women and children, but Petir spotted a few elderly men. One man appeared to be constructing a bow similar to the one Maid Rianne carried. A couple of children were lugging water toward a cooking pot suspended over a fire. Several women were working on some kind of animal hide stretched across a frame. A couple of spinning wheels merrily whirled away, the spinners tracking the approach of Petir's stretcher with curious expressions. The sounds of metal banging on metal drifted from the far end of the encampment. An anvil?

A shapely woman left her seat by a cooking pot and stomped toward the returning party.

"Cordelia! Where is your dress?"

Cord shrugged at Maid Rianne and trotted off. "I was remiss, Mother. I shall don it directly."

*Cordelia? Cord is a girl?* Petir surreptitiously tried to check out the other boys.

The one called Will caught his eye and winked. "Aye, m'lord, *we* all be lads," he confirmed with a chuckle.

Petir returned a feeble grin before he resumed his survey of the encampment. Too bad his environmental science prof couldn't see this. She was a middle-aged woman who bounced on her toes when she got excited about her topic. Although he had accidently registered for the class, her enthusiasm had made him stay.

This camp had no electricity, no running water, none of the comforts of modern civilization. These people were living off the land, which apparently provided them with what they needed, including a place to hide out. It was awesome. His prof would be jumping up and down like a nut.

A whiff of something good drifted on a breeze from the general direction of the cooking pots. His stomach rumbled in response.

*Wow, this is some dream!*

\*\*\*

## Chapter 5: Unmaidenly Thoughts

The pot of salve still reeked, although Rianne's hands were now dry in the evening air. With a guilty start, she stomped in annoyance. How long had she been standing there with that smelly salve like the village idiot?

*Long enough.*

"Silly girl. 'Twas merely a moment's reaction. You have not betrayed Lord Robert's trust." She slammed the cover back on the pot. "Not that he deserves it." They would reconcile, and things would go back to the way they were before. They would bask in mutual admiration, and she would hide her love of archery.

But remembering the stranger's intense regard made her pulse quicken slightly. She was unaccustomed to such open, raw admiration. She felt sheepish at the pleasure she had experienced when the stranger's mouth had fallen agape as he watched her walk. Of course, her weaponry might have prompted his reaction. She played back the encounter. No. His admiring regard had been solely for her. She paused again, her mind once more preoccupied with definitely unmaidenly thoughts of the newcomer.

With a twinge of guilt, she reminded herself again she was pledged to Lord Robert Gisborne. *I am certain he would respond in a similar manner under similar circumstances. And I would react to him as I did the stranger.* Irrefutably, her reaction had been innocent.

Besides, the newcomer could not compare with the strong and courageous Lord Robert. Broad and muscular under his chain mail and leather, her knight was skilled with both spear and lance. With his blond hair and grey eyes, he turned the head of many a maiden. Rianne was blessed he had chosen her. Why would she ever look at another, especially someone like Lord Petir, whose only skill seemed to be falling out of trees?

The newcomer was tall, almost lanky, like a youth who had grown too fast. He seemed awkward, both in movement and social skills. He was not handsome, but his eyes were a most unusual olive-green with a fringe of dark lashes. And when he stared at her from under that mop of shaggy, dark auburn hair, she felt unique. His hands were unused to hard labor, but his body had been firm and toned under her fingertips—

"I need a moment's respite where no one will find me."

Rianne jumped, guilt surging through her, as the wife of Fryer Tuck entered the tent. She Tuck winked at Rianne as she shook the mass of tawny curls already escaping the confines of her inept ribbon. Mistress Molly always had her hands full since the outlaw camp had fallen to her to manage. A gregarious husband and two active young boys yielded no measure of relief for the good-natured woman. Nevertheless, when Rianne had arrived, she had instantly taken her under her wing. Rianne owed her much.

"Good evening, Mistress Molly. You are always welcome." Embarrassed by her interrupted thoughts, Rianne hurriedly resumed her preparations to treat the newcomer, trying to hide the heat rising in her face, for the sharp eyes of the camp manager never missed a thing. "How do you fare this evening?"

"Well enough. Nothing a few moments of peace cannot cure. Running a camp is similar to running a home, but on a grander scale. And you, m'dear? Thinking of your beloved?"

"He is not my belov— Wait, who? Lord Robert? Of course! Why would I not? Of course I was thinking of Lord Robert."

Mistress Molly raised her brow. "Aye, of course you were. And how fares your stranger? Healer Aileen tells me he has strained a leg muscle."

"He is not *my* stranger. As her apprentice, I have been instructed to provide massage and a hot compress this evening, and nothing more."

"And nothing more? And what else would there be? After all, he is not what one would call handsome, is he?"

"Well, perhaps not handsome in the classic sense, but he is attractive in his own way." An image of Lord Petir's face flashed into Rianne's mind. "His smile is somewhat lopsided, but in an endearing manner. And his—"

Rianne broke off abruptly and frowned. She had walked right into that one.

"Mistress Molly, for shame! I am betrothed to Lord Robert! Lord Petir is my patient, nothing more."

"And no one is as handsome as Lord Robert."

Rianne laughed. "'Tis true enough." She sighed. "How I wish Lord Robert had chosen to live here instead of aligning himself with the sheriff."

"Aye, it would make things less confusing, would it not?" Mistress Molly's expression was far too innocent for her.

"I am not confused."

"Ahh, well, his courting the rich and powerful may do you well in the end."

"Nay, he should be defending the weak and innocent, not choosing to live comfortably off the labors of the oppressed. Why would he choose Prince John over King Richard?"

"Honestly, m'dear, at this point, the outcome between the battling royals matters not to me. I am tired of living outdoors, and tired of always being dirty."

"Aye, a decent bath will be my first duty after the royal conflict is resolved," said Rianne. "Although, if the truth be told, I will sorely miss being able to strap on a dagger."

Mistress Molly laughed. "Undoubtedly, it will not be permitted once you return to your home, whoever comes to rule the land."

"Do you think King Richard will succeed in his bid for the crown? His victory will mean forgiveness for every honest outlaw in this haven."

"Including thy transgressions as an 'outlaw-in-waiting'? Your betrothed expects a proper lady-in-waiting."

Rianne grinned, unabashed. She more than enjoyed the fact she was crossing social restrictions with her boyish garb and doing so without serious consequence. So far.

"The garments of a maiden are far too cumbersome for life in our hamlet," she said airily. "I am sure I will find a way to convince King Richard that Prince John and his promises confused Sir Gisborne, and he thusly deserves to be pardoned."

"Do not concern yourself with the outcome, m'dear. Should good King Richard be defeated, I expect you will still receive pardon through Lord Robert's influence with Prince John. You and he will simply return to your former life."

"Aye, but I expect no mercy from Prince John for those who befriended me when I escaped into the forest. He will not readily forgive those who abide here."

"'Tis true, I am certain, but we are much better off than poor Jocelyn."

Rianne scowled at the mention of the woman who had recently been taken by the sheriff's men, in front of her very small son, leaving behind a very angry husband and older boy. There was talk of trying to trade the newcomer for the unfortunate woman, especially since many in the camp suspected the stranger of having ties to the enemy.

Distracted, Rianne realized she washed her hands yet again before completing a sleeping draught for the injured intruder. She believed him sincere in his claims of injury, but she was determined to take precautions. Picking up a couple of soft cloths and the pot of salve, she headed for the healer's tent where, after Healer Aileen's more thorough examination and a meal of Fryer Tuck's hearty stew, their unwelcome guest bided. If the newcomer was attempting to ferret out their location for nefarious purposes, Rianne intended to discover his intrigue and put an end to him, no matter how nice his eyes.

\*\*\*

## Chapter 6: The Girl of His Dreams

"What's in it?" Petir sniffed the bowl suspiciously as he blinked the sleep from his eyes.

"Chamomile and brandy. It will soothe, m'lord," answered Maid Rianne in a mild voice.

"Brandy, huh?" This dream obviously did not take into account legal drinking age. He took a cautious sip, willing it not to burn his throat and embarrass him with a coughing fit.

"You having any?"

"Nay, m'lord. I do not need to be soothed." Smiling at him, she settled on the side of his sleeping pallet.

*Soooo! It was going to be that kind of dream.* Except for a couple of confused moments when he first awoke to Maid Rianne hovering over him, he was ready for whatever. Only in a dream would someone like Rianne come to his bed. He was not going to risk screwing up this dream with a stupid reality check. He gazed at her with open admiration, enjoying the combination of the heat her presence generated with the warmth of the brandy curling through his core.

"Are you comfortable, m'lord?"

"I am now." Only in a dream could a geek like him be bold with a lovely like her. Petir smiled at her and was surprised to see an answering blush. *He* had made her blush? Oh, yeah. He was loving this dream.

She made a little nervous gesture.

*A nervous hottie?* That was unexpected. Petir understood nervous all too well, and he certainly did not want the warrior princess feeling nervous. He gently captured her hand, and for a moment, enjoyed the cool softness of it. And because he had no idea what to do next, he raised it to his lips, reverently kissed it, and humbly returned it to her lap, his eyes never leaving hers.

She studied him quietly, looking oddly vulnerable, as if she were trying to decide what to do.

Petir gazed back unabashed, completely in awe of what he had just done. He was totally rocking this dream.

Maid Rianne moved her head the way Petir did when trying to clear cobwebs. She regarded him tentatively. "M'lord, I have come to see if I can make your rest more comfortable."

*Yes!* "What did you have in mind?" Petir encouraged. *Yes. Yes. Yes.*

"Well, I..." She leaned forward, resting one hand on his thigh, and steadying herself with the other. "I've been told I have a healing touch." She shifted her position so she could slide both hands under his thigh, gently finding and relieving his injured hamstring. Her palms began to slowly travel up his leg, kneading and stroking places he hadn't noticed existed, alternating between stimulating pain and easing it.

He took a hasty gulp of the brandy tonic in the bowl and tried not to jump on her. *Be cool. Be cool.*

As she worked, her body gently rocked in time with her massage. The cadence of his breathing somehow adjusted to match her movements.

Her dark hair curtained her face, robbing him of a much desired view. *Why not?* It was his dream. He reached up and secured the wayward hair behind her ear. She watched him, motionless, her eyes binding him as he slowly traced the long strands to their end.

Dream or not, he was astounded by the audacity of his conduct. It was like he couldn't help himself. He sat up, ignoring his aching body. Emboldened when she didn't retreat, he narrowed the distance between them. Cupping her head with one hand, he drew her near, pausing just inches from her mouth. He savored the closeness of her, feeling her breath, absorbing her warmth, not sure whether he dare proceed. *Jeez, this is just perfect.*

"Wait," she whispered breathily.

*Like hell.* He leaned into her, pressing his lips to hers. She received his kiss with a soft intake of breath, and then melted toward him. The unexpected weight of her body propelled him back onto the pallet. He landed with an awkward "oomph."

She lifted off him in alarm, her arms bracing her from both sides of his body as she hovered just inches away. Although they did not touch, their gazes locked them together as their ragged breathing blended with the night noises. Still she did not retreat.

That was enough of a signal for Petir. He propped himself up high enough to reach her mouth and waited. Her face tilted towards him, and he brushed her lips with his. *Now, that was a tingle.* Magically, she deepened their kiss. She was so warm, and—

"Be sure to check on our guest before you bed down," directed a male voice from outside the tent.

Maid Rianne's head shot up. Panic washed across her face as she scrambled to her feet, frantically tugging her clothing and smoothing her hair. The flap of the tent quietly opened, and a head popped in.

"All's well, Maid Rianne?"

"Yes, yes," she snapped. "Of course all is well, sir."

The intruder offered a puzzled look at her waspish tone as she self-consciously straightened her sleeves. He politely tipped his head at Petir, a suspicious glint in his eye. "Very well. Good evening, sir."

Petir shot a furtive glance at Maid Rianne, who avoided his eyes.

"One moment, sir, and I shall accompany you," she said, scooping up her belongings. And just like that, she was gone.

Dazed and elated, Petir flopped back on the pallet, all pain forgotten.

Maid Hottie had actually jumped his bones. Too bad you couldn't wrap it up in a box and put a bow on it. Now *that* would make a great birthday present.

*Best dream ever!*

## Chapter 7: The Land of Maid Hottie

Morning had come too soon. Petir dropped his arm across his eyes to maintain darkness as long as possible. The memory of kissing a fantastical warrior princess was fresh in his mind, her soft lips on his, her hair brushing his face. Too bad it had only been a dream. Unfortunately, the specifics were bound to fade as he became more awake, so he lay there in the early morning, eyes still shut, playing back the scene, and relishing the details. *You should be able to record a dream and save it for later.* He could get used to midnight visits from a medieval babe with a "healing touch."

*What is up with those birds?* For some reason, they were singing at maximum volume this morning. Willing the window to slam shut wasn't working. He didn't feel like getting up to do the deed himself, so his only other option, besides shooting them, was to ignore them.

Hoping for another crack at Maid Hottie, Petir tried to fall back asleep. Not only did the birds sound like they were belting it out in his very room, his bladder was completely unsympathetic when it came to sleeping in.

Petir yawned. Apparently, the universe was against him this morning. No doubt about it, he seriously had to pee, even at the risk of losing the Princess Hottie dream. He rolled over to check the time, and froze.

This was not his room.

It wasn't even a room. It was a tent. He wasn't even in a bed. He was on a pile of blankets. Staring around wildly, he shot up to a sitting position, pain shooting down his leg.

This could only mean one thing.

He was still in the land of Maid Hottie.
Both fists shot up over his head.
*YES*!

## Chapter 8: Wicked Ways of the Outlaw

Petir's eyes swung hopefully toward the opening tent flap. To his enormous disappointment, the head popping in was not that of a fair maiden. Instead, a cheerful smile accompanied the bewhiskered face and Irish brogue of Fryer Tuck.

"What ho, m'lord," Fryer greeted him. "Do ye feel up to a wee bit of food on this fine morning? As the chief cook, I can vouch for it."

"You're the cook? I thought you were a monk or something," Petir said.

"Aye, well, me name be Fryer Tucker, as in a frying pan, not as in a "friar" of the vows. No, I wouldna be a friar of the vows, would I, being wed to the fair Molly and proud father to Dale and Little John." Fryer Tuck's chuckle produced a grin from Petir.

"Oh, right. I'm not really up on that stuff."

"I be the best cook in these woods, m'lord, and that be the God's honest truth."

"*Methinks* you be the only cook in these woods," laughed Petir.

"Aye, m'lord, that also is most likely the truth." Fryer Tuck's smile broadened. "I have me galley set up pretty as ye please. Can ye be tempted?"

His mind turned to Maid Rianne. "Oh, most definitely. No doubt about it."

"Well, then, step lively, and I shall introduce ye to the wicked ways of the outlaw."

Petir attempted to stand but settled back on the pallet with an emphatic "Oomph!" He rubbed his hamstring tentatively. "I don't think there'll be any lively stepping from this body today," he said ruefully.

Fryer Tuck smacked his forehead with his palm. "Fool that I am! One moment, young sir." He disappeared, and returned shortly with a wiry older man bearing an armload of gray and tan clothing.

"May I present Gilbert Whitehand, Master Carver. Gil is our finest craftsman. Bows, arrows, staffs. He carves them all."

"M'lord." Gilbert gave Petir a nod and a craggy smile that matched his graying hair and goatee. "I hear you are in need of a crutch."

"I'd rather have one of those walking sticks to whip around."

Gil grinned. "Swinging a staff will come in good time, m'lord." He shook the clothing. "Perhaps you will allow me to provide you with a shirt and trousers more befitting than your current garb."

Petir surveyed his black polo shirt and cargo shorts, both of which had collected their share of grime as he had tumbled down the hill. "Yeah, they're pretty rank."

"You are more than welcome to these. You can wash yours at yonder brook, and hang them on a branch to dry."

Petir peeled off his shirt and shrugged on a gray cotton one. It settled on him like a tent. "Where did this come from?" He didn't need a mirror to tell him it was easily two sized too big. Fryer's expression of barely contained mirth told all.

"From none other than our blacksmith. He be a large man, that." Grinning widely, Fryer stepped forward to help Petir roll up the sleeves.

"He be a *very* large man," said Petir, imitating his Irish brogue. "I'm afraid to try the pants."

"Fear not, m'lord. I bear a vine that will make a very fine belt."

"A vine? Okay, whatever. So, where's this brook? The sooner I wash mine, the sooner I can put them back on."

"First, I must measure you for your crutch." Gil's face creased with humor. "Then you need to learn to walk with it. You will not be able to venture to the brook until then. You may find yourself garbed in this splendid attire for some time."

Fryer and Gil helped Petir to his feet. Gil proceeded to measure Petir from his armpit to his feet by counting the number of hand-spans.

"Hey, isn't that how you measure horses?" Petir asked.

"Similar, m'lord. Do you ride?"

Petir snorted. "If you count being a computer desk jockey."

When Fryer and Gil exchanged glances, Petir sighed. *They don't know what I'm talking about.* "Never mind. No, I don't ride."

"I have what I need," said Gil as he straightened up. "By your leave, m'lord." He bowed slightly, clapped Fryer on the back, and disappeared through the tent flap.

"It shall take him a couple of hours to complete the crutch. In the meanwhile, I shall fetch you a meal. Be back shortly, m'lord." Fryer ducked out of the tent.

Despite his injury, Petir managed to wrestle on the huge pants and secured them by knotting the vine around his waist. Rolling up the pant legs helped a bit, but it still looked like he was wearing a sheet. With nothing else to do, he lay back on the pallet. Through the tent he listened to the sounds of the camp coming to life in the early morning. The giggles of children mingled with the barking of a small dog. A woman, most likely their mother, was trying to round up Little John and Dale. It sounded like Cordelia's mother once again was attempting to get Cord to wear a dress. Someone began strumming a guitar and from farther off came the sounds of wood being chopped. Jovial banter surrounded the tent. A cheery flute eventually joined the guitar. Someone picked up their tune, singing as he walked by the tent:

> I'll go no more a roving with you fair maid
> A-roving, a-roving
> Since roving's been my rue-I-ay
> I'll go no more a-roving with you fair maid.

I kissed her once, I kissed her twice,
Mark well what I do say,
I kissed her once, I kissed her twice,
She said, "Young sir that's oh so nice."

*So these are the wicked ways of the outlaws. No wonder Robin Hood's men were so merry.* All and all, it sounded like a very satisfying way to live even if they were in hiding. There was only one thing missing... Maid Rianne.

Straining to hear her, Petir began to pick up the sounds of several arguing adults. He stilled. Apparently, he was the subject of their disagreement. They were heatedly debating whether they should let him remain in the encampment or deliver him to the nearest town.

*Leave the land of Maid Hottie?* Petir felt the stirrings of panic. *Oh, please. Not yet.*

\*\*\*

## Chapter 9: Keep Your Enemies Closer

Rianne bit her lip as she listened to the camp elders, all the while fingering a small keepsake hanging from her neck on a piece of yarn. As a younger member of the camp, it was not her place to join the heated discussion of the elders. Even if she could, what could she say after that inappropriate display in the healer's tent last night? She had shamefully kissed the stranger, and she was promised to another. It mattered not that she and Lord Robert had parted on bad terms. She should never have been tempted at all. She continued twirling the yarn around her fingers, winding and unwinding, spinning it like her thoughts.

Obviously, her judgment was compromised. Life would be far more simple if Lord Petir was gone, but the mere thought created a confusing hollow in her stomach. How could she have had any reaction to a complete stranger? Oh, how she wished he had never come to their forest.

"We don't know who 'e is or where 'e came from, Master Gil," snapped William Smythe, the blacksmith. "If you give him the crutch, 'e can move about as he pleases."

"So you suggest 'e remain confined to the healer's tent like a prisoner?" responded the always unruffled master carver as he idly twirled the half completed crutch in his hands. "And what if he is but an innocent traveler, ignorant of the conflict between the royals?"

"An important consideration, but William's point is also well made," said Ana, the elderly Gypsy who frequented their camp. She placed a calming hand on William's broad arm. "Anyone else?"

To Rianne, it seemed Gypsy Ana's musical accent relaxed everyone in the escalating disagreement. As the aging Gypsy looked expectantly at the others, they, too, spoke more calmly.

"Aye," chimed in Mistress Molly. "To confine 'im would be akin to abduction. We would become the outlaws they claim us to be."

"Aye, and more than just Prince John's soldiers would seek him," agreed William gruffly. "I still say we could trade him for my Jocelyn. The sheriff need not know he is but a traveler and not an outlaw."

Mistress Nellie nodded slowly. "Why not? 'E does not belong here. And we would know our camp is safe."

"The sheriff would take him prisoner," reminded Gil.

"Aye, but when he is released, he will be on the road that will lead him home," she replied. "What do you think, Gypsy Ana?"

The group turned toward her. The elders were fairly certain she was older than all of them—she had been traveling with the tournaments since before they could remember—but no one knew beyond a doubt, and none dared inquire. With her strange and mysterious gypsy ways, exciting some and making others uneasy, no one questioned her kindness, and all sought her for advice.

"While we cannot keep him prisoner, we know not who he is," said Gypsy Ana, her bright, brown eyes thoughtful. "Whether he be friend or foe, we should know who lives amongst us. As they say, keep your friends close, and your enemies closer."

William nodded vigorously. "Exactly."

"Fryer Tuck, that meal is for our guest, yes?" the Gypsy asked. "May I carry it to him?"

"Certainly." He handed the wooden plate to her.

"Very well. I shall meet this stranger and talk, yes? After I learn what there is to learn, we shall assemble at William's anvil an hour hence."

The others agreed. Rianne watch the group dispersing, her finger turning white under the tightly wound yarn. Gypsy Ana reached over to unwind the wooden token she had given Rianne.

"Mistress Nellie's beautiful spun yarn does not need any help from you, my dear, yes?" She laughed as she turned the girl by the shoulders. "Off with you. You come to blacksmith's tent with the others."

"You want me there, too?" Rianne asked in a low voice. She could not tell if she felt more relieved or alarmed, but, either way, discomfort nudged her.

"Of course, my dear. You are his healer, are you not?" Gypsy Ana flashed an enigmatic smile before she walked toward the tent that housed the source of everyone's angst.

*This healer needs to hit something.* Rianne grabbed her staff and headed for the practice area.

\*\*\*

## Chapter 10: Gypsy Ana

"You have less than a fortnight to win the fair maiden's hand."

Petir looked toward the tent entrance to find the accented words belonged to an old lady in a burst of colorful skirts. He watched her enter, a petite figure with smooth, olive skin at odds with her bright white hair. Whatever her age, she impressed him as being spry, energetic, and perhaps just a bit mischievous.

"Excuse me?"

"May I join you, m'lord? I bear your meal."

Petir automatically took the offered dish. "Sure. Thanks." He peeked at the plate. It certainly wasn't bacon and eggs. "What is it?"

"I believe it is fish and mushroom stew with dandelion greens, compliments of this great forest," she said as she carefully lowered herself to the floor to join him.

"Wild mushrooms? Dandelions?" Petir gave it a tentative sniff. It actually smelled pretty good. "Are they safe to eat?"

She leaned forward to press her thumb on his forehead then sat back. "No harm shall befall ye while under my protection, m'lord. I give you my word as a Gypsy."

"You're kidding, right? You're a real Gypsy? What was that thumb thing? Some kind of spell?"

"Only Gypsies understand the way of the Gypsy." She grinned and gestured toward his plate. "Eat."

"Fish stew for breakfast. You don't see that every day." It couldn't hurt to try it. After an inspiring first taste, Petir dove in. Minutes later, his initial hunger satisfied, he realized the elderly Gypsy sat quietly watching him eat. Embarrassed, he wiped a

hand on his pants and extended it. "I'm sorry. My name is Petir—
"

"P-e-t-i-r, no? Not P-e-t-e-r like the English. *Español, si?*"

"Yeah, my grandparents are *boricuas* from Puerto Rico, but I don't speak Spanish."

"Petir Rojo Capota," she said thoughtfully. "You know not the translation of your name, yes?"

He shook his head.

"Your grandparents, they are still living?"

"Yes. I live with them."

"Not you parents?"

"No." He paused. "They died when I was little."

She reached over and patted him on the cheek. "So lucky to have family to love you when they passed."

"Believe me, I know."

"Good." She slapped her thighs and prepared to stand. "When you return home, you will ask them what means your name."

Petir hurriedly put down his meal and reached out a hand to help her up. She accepted his help and patted his cheek a second time.

"You heart is good, m'lord, with no guile. If I were many years younger, I would be tempted myself."

"That's great." Petir snorted. "Explain that to the girls my age."

The Gypsy laughed. "No wonder she is confused by you."

"What? Who is confused?" Was she referring to Maid Rianne?

"It is of no importance, m'lord." She walked to the tent flap.

"Wait a minute. Who are you?"

"I am no one of consequence, m'lord. They call me Gypsy Ana. I have the kissing booth at the fair in the village. The English would call me a matchmaker."

"Are you? Because I sure could use one."

"I am simply a Gypsy trying to make an honest living."

"Oh, really?"

She gave him a mischievous wink and opened the tent flap.

"Wait a minute," said Petir. "Who were you talking about before?"

"Before, m'lord?"

"When you first came in."

"Ahhh, yes, before." She stepped back into the tent, dropping the flap. "You have less than a fortnight to win the fair maiden's hand."

"Who? Maid Rianne?"

She chuckled. "How many fair maidens do you know? Enjoy your meal, m'lord. Fare thee well."

"Hold up. What happens in a fortnight? Does she ride off into the sunset with the sheriff?"

"Close, m'lord. She is desired by one who seeks to be indispensable to sheriff."

"Desired?" That sounded bad. Maid Rianne with another guy? Petir's geeky heart stilled. That sure would make this a sucky dream.

Under the Gypsy's scrutiny, Petir cleared his throat. "Well, of course someone desires a Twinkie like her."

Gypsy Ana leaned over and took Petir's hand in hers. "She is a lost pawn unless you help her."

"*Me*?"

The tent flap opened, interrupting them. Master Gil popped his head in with a cheerful grin.

"Your pardon, m'lord, but 'tis completed."

"What?" Petir was having trouble switching gears between the two conversations.

"Your crutch, m'lord. You will now be able to move about on your own." The master carver smiled broadly.

"Well, then," smiled the Gypsy, once again heading for the entrance of the tent.

"Wait! Wait! What did you mean?" Petir asked her.

"With a little thought, m'lord, you shall figure it out, no? But now, the master carver craves an audience, so I shall be on my way. Good day to you, m'lord, and to you, Master Gil." She gave them both a bright smile and disappeared out of the tent.

Confused, Petir sagged onto the pallet.

*How long is a fortnight anyway?*

## Chapter 11: Have Crutch, Will Travel

"Gil, you have some serious skills." Petir inspected his ticket to mobility. Smooth to the touch, it was shaped like the letter Y at the top and was widened slightly at the bottom. Gil hauled Petir to his feet. Slipping the fork under his armpit, Petir inhaled the new-wood smell.

"Many thanks, young sir. However, opposite arm from the injury," instructed Gil. "The wider base will afford you a bit more stability."

Petir shifted the crutch to his other side and took a tentative step. With the crutch bearing most of his weight, the pain shot down his hamstring with far less intensity.

"Nay, lad. Good leg and crutch move together. Bad leg moves with a short step while the staff and your good leg bear your weight."

"Ohhh." Petir adjusted his stance, his movements awkward as he tried to protect his injury. "I get it. Yeah, that's way better."

"Shall we take this outside, m'lord?" Gil held the tent flap open.

Petir took a couple of tentative steps outside where the sunlight streaked through the mist of early morning. *Success.* "Now that's what I'm talking about."

*Crutch Equals Mobility. Mobility Equals Finding Rianne*

He took another couple of steps and grinned widely at Gil. "I'm going to check this place out."

"Your patience, m'lord. There is more." Gil had a roguish glint in his eye. Insuring Petir would not topple, he took the crutch and stepped away, spinning it between his palms. With a lunge so sudden Petir had no time to jump, the master carver slammed the fork of the crutch neatly into the ground between Petir's feet.

"Whoa," breathed Petir. "Am I the only person here who can't do that?"

"It takes a little practice," Gil acknowledged modestly.

"Yeah, plus coordination and lightning reflexes."

"You said you wanted a staff, m'lord." Gil passed it back. "And you need a crutch. You now have both."

Petir assumed an infomercial voice. "*A weapon and a tool in one.* Now, *that's* convenient."

*Crack!* A rock bounced off the tree next to him.

"Anything can be used as a weapon, m'lord," called a redheaded kid from across the clearing. It was Cord, AKA Cordelia-Without-A-Dress. A piece of cloth dangled in her outstretched hand.

"I see you have evaded your mother again." Master Gil smirked as she sauntered over.

"Did you use that cloth as a slingshot?" asked Petir.

"Yes, I did, m'lord."

"Cool. Can you show me how?"

"At your service." Cord reached an admiring hand to stroke the crutch. "A thing of beauty, Master Carver."

"My thanks, m'lady." Gil tipped his hat at her.

"C'mon. Let's try this baby out," said Petir. Time to make Jackie Chan proud.

"By your leave, Master Carver," Cord said politely.

"Yes, yes, by your leave, Master Carver," parroted Petir. "And thanks a lot."

Smiling, Gil tipped his cap one last time, and headed to the group conversing with the little old Gypsy in her colorful skirt.

Petir hobbled around the side of the hill after Cord. He was about to get him some skills with his new toy.

## Chapter 12: Warriors and Idiots

"Ow!" Petir rubbed his arm and glared at Cord, who was glaring back.

"You are not supposed to let me hit you."

"*I know* I'm not supposed to let you hit me. I'm not an idiot."

"That remains to be seen," muttered Cord. "You are definitely not a warrior. If you cannot defend yourself, simply say so." She spun her staff between her hands.

"Of course I can defend myself. I just wasn't ready. Try again." Petir had played Wii Karate before, and he was ranked at Ping-Pong. This warrior stuff couldn't be too hard, especially against a middle-school girl who only came up to his chest. He raised his crutch over his head with one hand and extended his free arm in front of him like a cop trying to stop traffic. Bending his knees slightly, he ignored the pain shooting up his hamstring as his tent-clothes flapped in the breeze.

Jackie Chan would be proud.

"Go for it," Petir told the girl, shifting his weight onto his good leg.

Cord shot him a disgusted look as she viewed his position. Without changing her stance, she tossed her staff into one hand and thrust it into his midsection. Petir dropped like a sack of potatoes.

Jackie Chan would not be proud.

"Right." Cord stood over him for a moment. "Warrior or idiot? Hmmmm. Difficult choice." Scowling, she tossed her staff on the ground next to the gasping Petir, stepped over his prostrate form, and stalked off. "Now I must fetch the 'ealer. I wager she will be telling me mum about this, and I shall never hear the end of it."

"The 'ealer's apprentice is here. And I will be telling your mum about what, exactly?"

Petir tried to respond to the sound of Maid Rianne's voice, but his gut had not yet loosened. Her foot under his shoulder deftly rolled him onto his back. *Wow, she looks good in the morning.* His lungs were slowly returning to normal, at least normal enough for him to feel embarrassed.

"Tell your mum what?" she repeated, arching a brow at the shamefaced Cord.

"That I—"

"That I …tripped…on my…crutch," Petir hurriedly interjected between wheezes. "She thought it…was funny." He wasn't trying to keep Cord out of trouble so much as he was downplaying getting beaten up by a girl. Whatever. If he could help her out in the process, so be it.

"Aye? Then why be ye gasping like a fish out of water?"

"Because I…fell on my stomach." *That sounds lame.*

Apparently Cord agreed, judging from the eyeballs rolling around in her head.

Maid Rianne surveyed the two of them. "Mmm-hmmm. As you wish." She jerked her head toward the camp. "Are you not supposed to be helping the good Fryer Tuck, Cord?"

The younger girl opened her mouth in protest, but Maid Rianne's stern expression silenced her. "Aye, m'lady." Cord gave Petir a grateful glance and ran off, grumbling about women's work.

"Do not let Fryer Tuck hear you speak so," Maid Rianne called after her with a grin.

Petir sat up, and Maid Rianne leaned over to help him. He winced as she grasped his upper arm where Cord had landed her first blow. He winced again as Maid Rianne hauled him to his feet and pain shot down his hamstring. She steadied him as he hopped on his good leg. Regaining his balance, he gingerly rubbed his stomach.

"Serves you right, m'lord." She folded her arms across her chest and glared. "Did I not tell you to rest your leg? You will heal faster."

"Yeah, you and the master healer both." Healer Aileen's orders were to stay put for the rest of the day, but the crutch fashioned by the master carver had been his ticket to roam, and he couldn't resist the temptation. Maid Rianne needn't know he had been hoping to run into her.

She retrieved the discarded staff and his crutch. Testing the heft of the crutch, she spun it in her hand, her features softening. She stopped the spin and returned it to Petir.

"Aye, no reason a crutch could not serve as a weapon." Her expression held an impish glint. "But your strange stance leaves you open to attack." She struck an imitation of his martial arts pose, made all the more ridiculous by the bow and quiver of arrows adorning her body.

"Oh, you saw that."

"Aye, I saw that. And the memory shall help me get through the long, desolate winter nights." She was grinning at him. She had a great smile.

Suddenly he felt cocky. "Yeah, well then, why don't you give me a lesson on how to use one of these things. Everyone seems to know how except me." *What better way to get some quality alone-time with Maid Hottie?*

"Surely, you jest. Now is not the time, not with your injury."

"Even injured people need to know how to defend themselves…and don't call me Shirley." He waited.

Maid Rianne blinked at his pun and burst into laughter.

Maid Rianne the Huntress, was breathtaking. Healer Rianne was temptation personified. But laughing Rianne enchanted.

His mouth was once again agape, but he couldn't help it. Her head thrown back in the morning sun as merriment burst from her throat took his breath away. Too bad she wasn't a real person and this was only a dream because Petir had found his purpose in life—to make Maid Rianne laugh.

He snapped his mouth shut as she recovered.

"You were right, m'lord. You are indeed clever." She contemplated Cordelia's staff. "'Tis true even the injured must be able to protect themselves." Reaching a decision, she lifted her quiver from around her chest and dropped it, along with the bow, into the leaves.

"A lesson on being a warrior, then."

*Yes! Yes! Yes!*

## Chapter 13: Rianne, the Warrior

*Be cool. Be cool. Who knows where this can lead. Be cool. Be cool.*

Petir schooled his features into what he hoped reflected diligent interest as Maid Rianne paced in front of him. She cleared her throat and came to a stop.

"Well, then. For a novice, the approach should be to command thy balance and read thy opponent. Anticipation will be your greatest defense." She began by demonstrating how to lower his center of gravity by bending his good leg and extending the debilitated limb to the side, where it became a support instead of a liability.

He should be concentrating on her words, but he was completely distracted by her presence. He resorted to the old standby—humor. With his injured leg extended to the side, Petir struck a karate pose with his staff raised overhead and his free hand weaving ominously in the air.

"Ooohwwwaaaaahhhhh."

Maid Rianne blinked at his Bruce Lee imitation for a moment. Then, ignoring the interruption, she continued teaching him how to defend himself.

He sheepishly straightened up to watch her repeat the blow she had landed next to his head at their first encounter. She rained the blow around his feet again and again until he could read the exact moment she was going to strike. She also imitated the two blows struck by Cordelia—yes, she had seen the entire scene—until he could anticipate those strikes as well.

Petir was getting impatient with the lessons but was not sure how to press the fast forward button on his dream. He resigned himself to admiring the way her agile body moved around him. He silently congratulated himself at being caught gaping at her only three times, but it was getting harder to concentrate on her instruction.

Maid Rianne's exertions brought a rosy sheen to her cheeks. A few loose hairs had begun to curl around her face. Her confidence and strength captivated him completely.

"Now, for your hands." She shifted to stand behind him. Barely as tall as his shoulder, she had to reach around his body to align the staff in his grip. "Should an enemy..." Petir could hear the smile in her voice, "even a *small* enemy...thrust her staff at your midsection, you position your staff thusly." She stood behind him with her arms overlapping his, guiding his hands to their proper spots.

*Okay, here we go. Be cool. Be cool.*

She leaned into him so he could get a better feel for his center of gravity, but all he noticed was her warmth on his back. *Now that's what I'm talking about.* This was better than he had been hoping for. With a bit of imagination, it felt a little like she was hugging him.

Petir had a lot of imagination.

Maid Rianne walked around to face him, making adjustments as she moved, changing the angle of his elbows, smoothing his shoulders to a more relaxed pose. Facing him, she covered his hands with hers, nudging them to a better spot along the staff. Hers were smooth and strong, but so much smaller, making his seem like bear paws.

Her touch made Petir all the more aware her lips were less than a foot away, just on the other side of the crutch. The urge to kiss her was becoming increasingly distracting. He weighed his options while trying to concentrate on her lesson then reached a decision.

*What the hell. It's my dream. I can do what I want.*

Maid Rianne's lesson was currently providing him with a clear view of her profile. Leaning over the crutch, he gently nuzzled her cheek.

She jumped, indignantly whipping her head toward him. "What are you do—"

He stopped her from stepping back and captured her lips before the words were out of her mouth. She froze, and he tensed. Tactical error?

Then, miraculously, she melted, all compliant and yielding, and kissed him back. He nudged her mouth open with his gentle explorations. Amazed at his brashness, he gave himself over to the wonder of the moment. Her lips were impossibly soft, and she smelled incredible. He clearly had to draw her closer.

The forgotten crutch fell from Petir's hands, painfully smacking his good shin. The noise startled them both back to reality. Despite the pain, he managed not to grab his ankle and hop around. Too late; the spell had been broken and reality was rapidly settling in. They stared at each other, both breathing irregularly. Her cheeks flamed, evidence of her fluster.

*Unbelievable.* He, Petir Rojo Capota, had flustered the resident hottie.

"This is not appropriate, m'lord." Maid Rianne stepped back out of range.

"Wait. Sure, it's appropriate. We're both consenting adults, aren't we?"

"I am not consenting."

"It's only a phrase. I mean…I meant…. How old are you, anyway?"

"I am soon to be eighteen, m'lord."

"Great. That's great. I just turned nineteen. No problem there."

"There *is* a problem, m'lord. I must insist this behavior cease immediately."

"No, no, no, no." Petir was panicking. The Perfect Moment was fading, quickly transforming to the growing intensity of the Desperate Moment. "It's all good. We're just learning about each other."

"I have learned enough from you," she snarled. "Let us see what you have learned from me." She scooped up his crutch and grabbed Cord's staff.

*Whoa. She's mad.* His ego deflated as her reaction registered.

"Prepare to defend yourself!" Maid Rianne shoved his crutch at his chest.

She grabbed Cord's staff near the end with both hands and whirled around. Her first swing was at his head. Instinctively, he dropped down into a protective stance, the hairs on the top of his head quivering in the wake of her staff. She smoothly spun in a circle, twirling the staff overhead. He saw her weight shift and reacted, blocking her downswing with the crutch held over his head. She followed with a horizontal swipe, stopping short of his unprotected ribs.

*Whoa. That would have hurt.*

She stepped back, breathing deeply, her face flushed. He stood up, panting much less gracefully than she.

"Your lesson is concluded, m'lord. There is nothing more you need to learn from me." Maid Rianne snatched up her quiver and bow. The quiver she slung over her shoulder, but she brandished the bow, waving it toward his nose as if she held a sword.

"Heed my words, m'lord. There will be no other indiscretions." She spun on her heel and stormed back to camp.

Petir watched her go as he repositioned the crutch under his arm, feeling dazed and elated. For a day that had begun with him getting beaten up by a middle-school girl, all in all, this had been a great morning. After all, he had just spent a good hour in combat training with Maid Hottie. Throughout, it had been perfectly appropriate for him to openly stare at her, uncensored. When she had moved in close to show him how to stand, he had kissed her, *and* she had kissed him back, *and* when she went all Warrior Princess on him, he had actually used his new staff to defend himself.

If Maid Hottie thought he wasn't going to try for another indiscretion after all that, she was crazy. It was his dream, and he was going to 'indiscrete' every chance he got.

Now, where was Cordelia? He wanted a rematch.

## Chapter 14: Eating Like an Outlaw

Petir followed his nose to Fryer Tuck's galley where he found three fires being manned by Fryer Tuck and two men in their late thirties. One stirred a caldron hanging over the middle fire. The other was pouring water into another. Fryer Tuck tended some kind of meat on a spit over one of the fires while Cordelia prepared vegetables.

"You seem to have adjusted well to the ways of the outlaw," observed Fryer Tuck.

"So have you," said Petir. "This is some setup you got here."

"Aye. Well, it took a bit to get it to my liking. 'Tis not easy to cook for a camp full of outlaws."

"You cook for the whole camp?" Petir surveyed the galley. "Here?"

"Aye, that I do."

"How many people are there?"

"Not quite sixty. I have more help with the larger meals. The menu is never the same. It depends on what the forest yields, but it be a labor of love."

"That's amazing."

"If you be amazed by that, you should meet me wife, Molly. She organizes the entire camp." Fryer's pride was unmistakable. "She makes sure all are fed, clothed, and sheltered."

"Aye," chimed in Cord. "And she organizes the outlaws, too. She sets up the hunting parties, the foraging parties...."

"Aye, and she makes sure all the craftsmen have all the help they need." Fryer nodded toward Cord with a grin. "Back to your task, girl."

"Wow. She does all that by herself?" Petir was impressed. He couldn't even organize his two roommates into coming on vacation with him.

"Mistress Nellie and Mistress Aileen help her, but 'tis me Molly who be the backbone of the camp."

Petir sniffed longingly, his earlier meal completely forgotten. "That smells great. What are you cooking?"

"The hunters brought down a deer yesterday," answered Fryer.

"Not a very healthy specimen," said the man with the now-empty water bucket. He swung the caldron over the flames and wiped his hands, chuckling. "'Tis most likely the reason they were successful at all, but it will be tasty nonetheless."

"It sure smells tasty," said Petir.

Fryer chuckled and produced a knife. He swung the spit away from his fire and carved a few slices off the meat. Using the butt of the knife, he shoved the meat back over the flames. He passed out slices of meat to Petir and the other cooks and winked. "Privileges of courting the cook's favor."

Cordelia joined Petir as he maneuvered to sit on the ground. Blowing on his fingers, he managed to get a bite without dropping it.

"This sure tastes like it was a healthy specimen. What did you put on it?"

"Garlic and chives," said Fryer, his own mouth full. "One of the womenfolk had the foresight to bring garlic with her when she joined us."

"The chives grow wild in the grassy knolls," added Cord, licking her fingers.

"How do you know the deer wasn't healthy?" asked Petir.

"She was too thin, and she had disease bumps in her hide," replied Cord.

"That is what comes from protecting the herd instead of letting them be hunted," said Fryer. "Their numbers grow too large, and their food supply canna support them."

"Here it comes. Brace yourself, m'lord," intoned Cord.

"'Tis not like when humans who do not have enough food," continued Fryer. "When the royals keep the wealth for themselves, only the poor do not get enough to eat. But deer do not hoard like people do. If one deer is going hungry, most likely the entire herd is hungry. If this deer…" he tilted his head at the spit, "is any indication, this herd will have a difficult winter."

"Do not get him started, m'lord," snickered Cord. "He can preach all day about the proper balance of nature."

Fryer Tuck ruefully rubbed his beard. "Aye, that I can. That I can."

"But he's right, Cord," said Petir. "You can't mess with Mother Nature. She has her own balance going just fine. I read about this place where they killed off all the wolves to protect the deer. Without predators, the herd got so big, they ate all the vegetation and began to starve. Then the birds and rodents disappeared because there was no cover for them anymore, so the hawks and eagles had no prey. With the grass gone, there were no roots to hold the soil in place, so the rainstorms eroded the dirt into the streams and ruined the fish habitat. They are trying to reintroduce the wolves to the area, but the best they can hope for is that a new balance will be established, because the old one is permanently destroyed."

Petir stopped and felt his face grow warm. His audience was staring at him with a variety of expressions. Fryer Tuck looked delighted. The other two men were regarding him with respectful surprise. Cord was rolling her eyes.

"Oh no, not two of you," groaned Cord.

"I'm just saying," Petir amended.

"Mind your manners, Miss Cordelia," said Fryer. "His lordship is one-hundred percent correct. You would do well to learn from him."

"Actually, I wanted to learn from her," said Petir. "I'm here looking for a rematch." He began tossing his crutch from hand to hand, issuing a silent challenge to Cord.

She sniffed and tossed her head. "Not until you learn to defend yourself, m'lord. It will not bode well for me if I flatten you a second time whilst you are still injured."

The other cooks walked over to sit with them. The man who had been stirring the simmering pot extended his hand to Petir. "James the Potter. Well spoken, young sir."

"Thanks."

"So you are the odd game the young foragers brought back yesterday." James took bite of his meat slice.

"Yup, that would be me. You're the potter? A potter who stirs a pot?" Petir smirked.

"Aye, that be my lot in life today," James acknowledged with a grin.

"Do not be so modest, potter," said the other cook. He leaned over to shake Petir's hand. "Tanner is the name, m'lord. I work with leather." He gestured toward James. "His skill with the wheel is unparalleled. 'E produces the finest pottery in the land, and with clay from the floor of this very forest."

"Wait. You make your own clay? How do you do that?" Petir asked.

"For what we have here, the easiest way is to stir soil into water and let it settle. The clay particles are very fine, you see. They form their own layer and can be separated. At my shop, the task is made easier by the use of filters."

"So, at home, you're a potter, but here, you're a cook? What's in your pot?"

"Nay, I merely serve the cook. 'Tis me duty for today."

"We rotate responsibilities, m'lord, old and young alike," said Tanner as he contentedly munched on his piece of venison. "He cooks a pot of porridge, enough to feed the camp. I will be cooking a soup from the meat and vegetables gathered today."

"Porridge?" That did not sound appetizing at all. Curious, Petir hauled himself to his feet and hobbled over to peer into the caldron.

"Give 'er a stir while you are there, if you do not mind, m'lord," said James, relaxing against a tree.

Petir retrieve a huge wooden spatula lying across the top of the pot and peered in. Porridge turned out to be oatmeal. "Porridge," he repeated. "Huh. Go figure."

"Would you like to try some? Sweetened with a bit of treacle, 'tis quite good," said Cord as she stood up.

"Aye, try it," encouraged Fryer.

*Treacle?* "Sure," said Petir. "I'll try anything once."

Wiping her hands on her pants, Cord fetched him a wooden bowl and then returned to her work. Treacle turned out to be sugary syrup. Petir rejoined the others sitting under the tree and blew on his steaming bowl of porridge.

"That pot is huge.

"We provide for fifty-eight outlaws," said Fryer.

"Fifty-nine," corrected Tanner with a nod in Petir's direction.

"So, you cook for everyone, you make leather, and you make pottery," Petir said, pointing to each man in turn. "What does everyone else do around here? Rob from the rich and give to the poor?"

"Nay, m'lord. Everyone must contribute something or the camp will not work," said James. "Some of us gather firewood and food, and others hunt. We work on our skills with the bow and staff in our free time. Everyone takes a turn at washing and cleaning. We are fortunate to have amongst us a blacksmith, and a tanner who is also a boot-maker." He nodded toward his friend.

"The young divide their time between foraging in the forest and assisting those in charge of the camp," said Cord. "Every night, Mistress Tuck assigns the chores for the next day."

"Me Molly has this camp in fine form," said Fryer proudly. "Aye, fine form, indeed."

"This morning, I help the good Fryer, and, this afternoon, Mistress Nellie." Cordelia looked up from the vegetables she was slicing. "She is the head spinner. You should see her turn sheep's wool into the finest yarn."

"Seriously? The only wool I've seen is in a sweater. I'd like to see that."

"You are welcome to join me, m'lord." Cord beamed at him. "We can go as soon as I finish my work here. Of course, many hands lighten the load, do they not?" she blatantly hinted.

"What? You want me to help you?" Petir taunted. "I thought I heard someone say that was woman's work."

"Woman's work?" roared Fryer good-naturedly.

"J.K. Just kidding. Sure I'll help." Petir lurched to his feet and dusted off his palms.

"You cut, and I'll wash," instructed Cord.

Petir peered into the huge wooden bowl to find a variety of greens, roots, and mushrooms. "Where did all this come from?"

"We find many things in the forest besides you." There was that mischievous smirk again.

He sifted the veggies through his fingers and held up a tightly curled green with a fuzzy brownish cover. "What are these?"

"Fiddleheads. They be young ferns. 'Tis past their season. We were lucky to find these."

"You eat ferns?" asked Petir. *Gross. This is the kind of babble you'd expect from a dream.*

"Just peel off the outside and cook. They make for fine eating," said Fryer over his shoulder.

"Sure they do. I suppose you can eat these, too?"

Cord looked to see what he was holding. "Milkweed stalks."

"Milkweed? You mean that plant with all the white fluffy stuff?" *Oh, yeah, dream-babble going on here. Absolutely.*

"Yes, but you canna eat the mature plants. Only the young shoots are edible," said Fryer. "You had them in this morning's stew."

"I did?" Petir took a moment to survey his stomach. He patted his belly. "Seems okay. Just don't tell me there were any frogs in there."

"Frogs? No, there were no frogs in there, but—"

Petir interrupted Fryer by raising his hands as if warding off the cook's words. "Stop. Really. I don't want to know. Just tell me what you want me to do, and I'll do it, but spare me the details."

## Chapter 15: By Invitation Only

"We crave an audience, young sir," called James the Potter.

Petir had hung out with him earlier that afternoon after wandering around in search of Maid Rianne. Apparently, the potter could create just about anything on a potter's wheel. With his encouragement, Petir had taken a turn at a spinning lump of clay. His attempts reminded him of summer camp as a kid. Back then, all of his creative attempts, whether they were cups, plates, or vases, had ended up as ashtrays for his *abuelos*, who did not smoke.

Petir paused in mid-hobble as the group with the potter approached. While he recognized a few, namely Gypsy Ana, Mistress Molly, and William the Blacksmith, some were new faces.

"We, the elders of the camp, have met with Mistress Aileen, the master healer," said the potter. "She judges you well enough healed to travel. If you wish it, we can put you on the path to the nearest village."

Petir's heart stilled. *Leave Maid Rianne? This would be a stupid dream without her.*

"However, we would invite you to stay and live among us," said Mistress Molly as the manager of the camp.

Petir's heart leapt. *Yes, yes, yes.*

"But be forewarned," she cautioned. "To stay means you willingly consort with outlaws and, in doing so, will be declared one yourself."

"Aye, 'tis regretful but true." The old Gypsy wagged her head.

"'Tis also true that to join us, you must live as we live and eat as we eat, surviving off the land," added William.

"Know that this life will not last forever," warned Mistress Molly. "It cannot, and, believe me, the end is coming sooner than you think with the inevitable conclusion of the battling royals. But until we are forced from this land, we invite you to stay with us and lead the merry life."

"Yes. Oh, yes. I want to stay here with you and lead the merry life," Petir echoed emphatically as relief coursed through him. *I can be plenty merry with Maid Rianne around.*

"'Tis settled, then," said Mistress Molly. "But you cannot remain in the healer's tent. William Smythe, our good blacksmith, has offered to let you share the tent with his family."

William Smythe directed a curt nod at him.

*Right.*

"He has two sons," she continued. "You have already met Will, the eldest. His foraging party found you in the forest."

"Okay, sure. Thanks." *I'd rather bunk with Maid Rianne.*

William produced another curt nod.

Petir regarded the blacksmith's grim face. *I'll be staying out of his way as much as possible.*

"Then it is settled. We will bid you good day, young sir," said the potter.

"Aye, and welcome," added one of the men, clapping Petir on the back as the group began to disperse.

Gypsy Ana remained by Petir's side. "You turn outlaw for her, eh? Now you save the fair maiden, yes?"

"Save Wonder Woman? Hah! Trust me, there is nothing about that girl that needs saving."

"Ah, then she has shown you everything but her heart." The Gypsy tapped her chest knowingly and turned away.

Maid Rianne's disappointingly hasty retreat the previous night popped into Petir's mind. He snorted and muttered, "Not everything."

Gypsy Ana looked back with a raised brow. He instantly felt hot under the collar. She might not understand his slang, but he needed to watch the sexual innuendos leaking out of his mouth. He definitely didn't want to make the mistake of talking like his roommates in front of his *abuela*.

"I mean she hasn't shown me how to use the bow and arrow yet," he amended.

"There is plenty of time for that tomorrow."

"Yeah, if tomorrow comes."

"Tomorrow always comes." Gypsy Ana patted him on the arm and walked away.

*Not if I wake up first.* It stood to reason he'd be waking soon. This dream seemed unusually long. What if he ended up not seeing Maid Rianne before it ended? That would suck big time. The idea made him feel…

*OMG, What am I doing? Am I crushing on Maid Rianne?* Suddenly Petir was experiencing a private moment of embarrassment. Some dream girl had actually stirred his interest more than any real-life girl. *You are lame. So very lame.*

*No, wait. I'm a normal American eighteen-year old— I mean, nineteen-year old.* He had to be just lusting after Maid Hottie.

*Lusting Equals Good*
*Crushing Equals Bad*

Actually, it didn't matter. Either way, it was ridiculous. *She's only a figment of your imagination.*

He seriously needed to start checking out the girls on campus. It was time to abandon the geek-shield developed after losing his parents. It had provided an effective buffer in middle-school but had become more than a habit in high school. Although Geekdom had served him well, he had vowed college would be different.

But, here he was, heading for his second year, and so far, the only thing different was this lame dream.

# Chapter 16: Not So Merry

"Hah!"

*Thwack!*

"Hah!"

*Thwack!*

"Hah!"

"Ow!" Petir vigorously rubbed the shin five-year-old Scottie Smythe had just smacked with his stick. "Take it easy there, champ." They had eaten breakfast together after spending the night in the Smythe family tent. Scottie had tagged along to the brook when he retrieved his dry clothing. Apparently, he now had a new best friend.

Ignoring Petir's discomfort, Scott continued to prance around, brandishing the stick as if it were a staff. Moisture glistened on his freckled face, and he had long since given up on keeping his cap perched on his curly blond hair.

"I am becoming really good at this, am I not, m'lord?"

"Yeah, well, I was a little distracted. Go ahead. Try it again."

Oh, yeah, Petir was more than a little distracted. Across the clearing stood Amazon Hottie with her bow and arrow, engaged in a little target practice of her own. Little did Scottie know, he was simply a pawn in Petir's brilliant plan to set himself up for another "indiscretion" with the currently standoffish maiden.

Yesterday had not provided any such opportunity. Maid Rianne had left the camp with a hunting party. When they had returned at dusk with a couple of pheasants and rabbits, she had promptly handed them over to Fryer Tuck and disappeared before Petir could hobble over. In early evening, Healer Aileen, a no-nonsense widow "extensively trained in the healing arts," had provided a massage for his injured hamstring. Despite his disappointment, Petir had taken advantage and pumped her for info on Maid Rianne, her apprentice.

Somewhere in the middle of the conversation, Petir had drifted off to sleep. He didn't even remember the Smythes coming into the tent, but there they were when morning broke. Since Petir still found himself in dreamland, he was doubly determined to steer today's events in a more satisfying direction.

Scottie enthusiastically resumed his attack. Petir leaned against a tree, parrying the blows with his crutch.

"Hah!"

*Thwack!*

"Hah!"

*Thwack!*

"Hah!"

"Ow! C'mon!"

"I told you I was becoming really good at this! Me mum will be so proud."

*A mother?* Evidently, Will and Scottie were not the blacksmith's only family. Besides Scottie's formidable father, there had been no mention of another parent. "Your mum? Where is she?"

Scottie stopped swinging his stick and stood solemnly in front of him. "The bad men took her, m'lord." Sorrow took command of the little boy's features as he began stabbing the brown leaf litter on the forest floor. "We were picking berries when they came. She hid me in the bushes and ran away, but they caught her." He stabbed another leaf. "They did not catch me. I was quiet as a mouse, just like me mum told me."

Petir did not know what to say as he watched the little boy begin to push leaves around with his toe.

"I miss me mum, m'lord. I try to be brave, but I miss her." Scottie's voice quavered.

Sympathy and panic surged in Petir. He didn't know how to comfort a little kid.

Scottie looked up, shining blue eyes betraying his effort to not cry. "Please do not tell me father. He is mad all the time now, and I do not want to make him any madder. He misses her, too, you see."

*Poor kid. No wonder William always looks like he is about to explode. I wouldn't want to make him mad, either.* Petir awkwardly patted Scottie on the shoulder, wondering what he should do if the kid started crying. The boy resumed regarding the ground, suspiciously sniffling.

"C'mon, hit me some more. You'll feel better," encouraged Petir.

Scottie swiftly backhanded his nose and hoisted his stick. "I must practice if I am going to rescue me mum." He resolutely set his small shoulders and raised his staff. "Defend yourself, m'lord, for I will show you no mercy! Hah!"

*Thwack!*

"Hah!"

*Thwack!*

"Hah!"

"Ow!"

"M'lord!"

"I know, I know. I'm not supposed to let you hit me." Petir ruefully rubbed the insulted shin.

"Scottie," called Will as he trotted around the bend. "Father wants you. He is firing the hearth and needs you to work the bellows." Will was like a larger version of Scottie, from the same blue eyes and blond curls right down to the splash of freckles across his nose.

"Truly?" Scottie pranced up and down with excitement. He bobbed in Petir's direction. "By your leave, m'lord. Father is going to teach me how to make a necklace for me mum for when she escapes."

He ran off, oblivious to the distressed look on his older brother's face. Will sighed and turned to go.

"Hey," said Petir, detaining the boy as Scottie darted around the bend. "I'm sorry to hear about your mother."

"Did *he* tell you?" Will nodded toward his departing brother.

"Yeah. Tough deal. Just so you know, he told me he's practicing with his staff so he can go rescue her."

Will sighed. "He has had nightmares since he saw her taken. We tried to explain it was just a game to help him to adjust." He set his features. "He is just too young to understand."

Petir nodded. "I heard last night. Poor kid." He looked at Will. *What do you say to a middle-school kid?* "How about you? How are you adjusting?"

Will frowned. "Me mum is gone. I must watch my little brother to keep him from trying to rescue her. My father is ready to bite everyone's head off. How would you be?" Will turned and headed for the tents.

Petir watched him go and heaved a sigh. *I guess not all is merry with the merry outlaws.*

\*\*\*

Rianne bit her lip as she sadly watched Will take leave of Lord Petir and trudge off. Since Mistress Jocelyn had been captured, that poor family's life in the forest had become so complicated. Rianne found the sympathetic droop exhibited by Lord Petir somehow oddly appealing. He was tenderhearted, that one.

Rianne realized she was staring at Lord Petir and squared her shoulders. *Not that Lord Robert would not be tenderhearted...if the opportunity presented itself. He simply has not had the opportunity.*

Rianne tried unsuccessfully to picture Lord Robert's broad shoulders drooping sympathetically. No, he would remain strong. And dependable. And....

*Most likely, Lord Robert would not care.*

And rightfully so.

*Most likely, Mistress Jocelyn found herself a guest of the sheriff because she wandered too far from camp. Lord Robert would have no tolerance for that type of foolishness.*

*And rightfully so...*

So why were Rianne's emotions mirroring Lord Petir's slumped shoulders?

Rianne grabbed her quiver and bow. She and Lord Robert were people of action. It was time to act.

\*\*\*

## Chapter 17: Maid Rianne Disappears

Remembering where he was, Petir abruptly straightened and cast a furtive glance around.

*I hope the Amazon didn't catch me acting like a sentimental boob.*

A quick scan of the practice area revealed Maid Rianne had already left. Relieved, Petir hobbled over to the target that had received her arrows. Every single one was on the mark. Was there anything that girl couldn't do?

Petir grinned. *I'm going to get me some bow and arrow lessons from the Warrior Princess. She'll show me how to hold the bow—we'll be all close and cozy—that should lead to a little indiscretion.*

Unfortunately, Maid Rianne had disappeared.

At least that's how it appeared to Petir as he hobbled from one end of the camp to the other. Although it was disappointing not to find her, it had been a very interesting hobble. Mistress Nellie had taught him about her craft while she was busily spinning brightly dyed wool into yarn. He learned way more than he wanted about the process, including which plants rendered the dyes, but it was worth it. She also confided Maid Rianne had no family in the makeshift hamlet, but the Tucks kept a protective eye on her.

He resumed his quest but came up empty. That sucked. Spying William, Petir considered checking out the ironworks. Knowing his wife had been abducted somehow made William appear less formidable. Nevertheless, Petir approached with caution. He eyed Scottie busily working the bellows, his little face flushed with effort. The heat being produced was almost uncomfortable with the warm summer air, but neither father nor son appeared to care.

"Hey, have you seen Maid Rianne?" Petir ventured to ask after watching their efforts for a few minutes.

"You won't find her around here. She is paying a visit to my wife."

"Your wife? I thought she was a pris—" Petir glanced at Scottie, busy with his task and ignoring their conversation. "I thought she was a guest of the sheriff."

"That she is, but Maid Rianne would not be dissuaded from carrying a message from Scottie to his mother. Aye, she be a feisty one, that."

"But what if she gets caught?"

William chuckled. "Not Maid Rianne."

"How do you know? She doesn't have some kind of invisible cloak, does she? I didn't think so. She *could* get caught."

"Anything is possible, m'lord. But even if she is caught, she will be safe enough. She can tell the guard she was trying to sneak in to see her betrothed. No harm will befall her."

"You shouldn't have let her go," said Petir.

"*Let* her go? M'lord, do you really think *I* had a say in the matter?" The blacksmith laughed, a big booming sound that erased his perpetual scowl. "*You* tell Maid Rianne what she should do and inform me how that works out for you."

\*\*\*

## Chapter 18: Maid Rianne to the Rescue

Rianne crept around the bushes bordering the forest. She had an easy view across the clearing to the edge of the fair. Unfortunately, anyone on the other side also had a clear view. The trick was to cross undetected. She had done it before. It just required patience and timing. She had no idea how to find Mistress Jocelyn, but Rianne was determined. She was not returning without delivering Scottie's message to his mother. Skimming the periphery of the fair, her lip grasped firmly between her teeth, she waited for her opportunity.

Everyone was decked in their finery—lords, ladies, and peasants alike. Disappointment rippled through her as she watched the tournament attendees. She had so wanted to participate in the archery competition, but the risk of drawing attention was too great. Her capture would put the entire camp of outlaws at risk.

But she had a more important, although seemingly impossible, mission right now.

*What if I fail to sneak into the fair? And once I get in, how am I going to locate Mistress Jocelyn?* Rianne willed herself to be calm. *First things first. Where is the best place to slip in?*

She scanned the edge of the fair, ignoring the scampering children, bypassing the men carrying sacks of feed and bales of hay, disregarding a burly blond lord stealing a kiss from a redheaded wench behind a booth, and...

*Wait. Is that...?*

It was. This could not have been any easier. Mistress Jocelyn was seated on a log behind one of the booths, her arms folded over her stiffly held chest as she scowled at a royally uncomfortable guard. He stood apart from her, leaning on his staff, apparently avoiding her contemptuous glare. Mistress Jocelyn said something to the guard, who threw up his free hand as if in frustration and turned his back on his prisoner.

*Perfect!* Neither the guard nor Mistress Jocelyn was facing Rianne. Wrapping Scottie's message around an arrow, she secured it with a piece of Mistress Nellie's brightly colored yarn. She stealthily darted to a closer position along the forest's edge. Fitting her arrow into the bow, she stood up and sent it whistling.

\*\*\*

Robert Gisborn smiled lazily at the flavor of the week, taking in her black leather bustier atop a Lincoln green skirt, the former which he was in the process of unlacing. Oh, how he loved the way the girls costumed themselves for the tournament. The pretty redhead might not have much between her ears, but she had plenty between the laces.

"Are you sure we will not get caught?" she teased. She was a little breathless, anticipating a romp behind the baker's booth with the bold lord.

"Aye, I am positive." He had used this secluded little spot before, and with any luck, would get to use it again. "If I know my, uh, mother, she will not venture into the fair until the archery contest. As long as we are prudent tomorrow, there will be no problem." He tugged on one of her laces as he leaned in to kiss her neck.

Robert's fingers froze as his eye caught movement along the forest's edge. *Was that…?*

It was. *Good Lord!* He had to get rid of the redhead, and fast.

"Perhaps…." Robert placed a possessive kiss on her full lips while his eyes scoured the forest. "Perhaps we should schedule a rendezvous next week, just to be on the safe side."

"As you wish, m'lord." The girl giggled. "What do you say to this same time next week at the Hearthstone Pub?"

"Sure, sure. That sounds great. The Hearthstone Pub. I will be there." He dug into his pocket and produced some money. "Why don't you get us something to eat, and I'll meet you at the jousting arena," he said as he clumsily attempted to refasten her garments.

"My, my, m'lord. Your appetites certainly change quickly." She tilted her head flirtatiously, but her eyes were puzzled.

"Just part of my charm, my dear." He kissed her hand. "I shall see you directly."

She withdrew her hand and bobbed an impudent curtsy. As she sashayed off, the way her gait emphasized her assets was not lost on him.

Robert heaved a sigh of relief and turned his attention to the problem at hand.

Maid Marianne had come to town.

\*\*\*

Although Rianne immediately dropped back into the bushes, she was able to verify her arrow had lodged in the ground between Mistress Jocelyn and the guard, both of whom had jumped up in alarm. The guard immediately charged at his prisoner, pinning her against a wagon, sheltering her with his body while holding his shield protectively in front of his chest.

"What in hell's name?" roared the guard. "What idiot let an arrow fly at a fair?"

"Nay," came the muffled voice of Mistress Jocelyn from behind his shoulder. "Look at the arrow. It has a message attached."

The guard's cry had drawn some attention, and a few people had gathered, trying to spot the source of the arrow. The guard cautiously stepped away from his charge. He and a couple of men walked toward the forest.

"Show yourself!" demanded one of the men.

"Aye, show yourself," quavered another.

"It was probably some village idiot," grumbled the first man, "but I shall report it to the authorities."

The guard said nothing. With one last scrutiny of the forest, he returned to his prisoner.

"What is it?" asked the guard gruffly.

His tone made Rianne peek through the bushes. The others had already dispersed, leaving only the guard and his prisoner. Mistress Jocelyn had unwrapped the message from the arrow and was holding it over her heart.

"'Tis a long time for a child to be without his mother." Her voice trembled as she held out the picture Scott had scrawled on a piece of cloth. "I miss them so."

The guard cleared his throat. "Well, 'tis the price you pay for choosing the life of an outlaw." He paused to clear his throat again. "Methinks I should report this to the sheriff. Most likely, he is going to be very angry and will ask me a lot of questions. It will probably take me some time to return. Mistress Jocelyn, you are to sit right there..." he pointed his staff at the log where she had formerly perched, "and wait for me. You are not to venture there..." he pointed his staff directly at the bush concealing Rianne, "into the forest while I am gone. Do I make myself understood?"

"Oh yes! Bless you, kind sir! I shall be exactly where you expect upon your return." Mistress Jocelyn gave him a kiss on the cheek, bustled over to the log, and obediently plopped down. The guard bobbed his head toward her with a conspiratorial smile and disappeared between the booths.

Mistress Jocelyn and Rianne sprang to their feet. Mistress Jocelyn gathered her skirts and scurried across the clearing. The two wrapped themselves into a fierce hug, scanned around for prying eyes, and dashed into the woods.

\*\*\*

*So my betrothed is rescuing the peasant woman.* Robert Gisborne smirked from behind a tent as he watched the two fugitives gleefully scamper into the woods. *Maid Marianne, your soft heart is going to lead me straight to the outlaw camp.*

He rubbed his hands together in anticipation of attaining that which all the prince's men had not been able to achieve. *I shall bypass the sheriff and go directly to Prince John with their location. He will see to it I am well paid, and I will still get Maid Marianne in the end.*

*And, next week, I have a pub to visit.*

\*\*\*

## Chapter 19: Predator and Prey

"Stop! Stop!" gasped Mistress Jocelyn. "This dress is too much for running on a hot summer's day."

"Aye." Rianne felt exhilarated by what she had just accomplished. "I shall expect your utmost support in future debates of proper maidenly garb."

Mistress Jocelyn enveloped her in a hug. "Am I truly free? Am I finally to return home to my boys?"

"Yes, all three of them." Rianne laughed as the two twirled. "Your two sons and the one you married."

"I imagine my William has been quite angry."

Rianne expressed confirmation with a most unmaidenly snort. "Your children have been better behaved!"

Mistress Jocelyn stepped back and took both of Rianne's hands in hers. "I shall never be able to repay you, my dear."

She opened her mouth to reply, but Mistress Jocelyn joggled her hands up and down. "Oh, let us make haste and be on our way!"

The former captive gathered her skirts with renewed energy and dashed toward home. Rianne followed, infused with Mistress Jocelyn's excitement.

\*\*\*

*Crack. Rustle, rustle. Crack!*

No matter how hard he tried to move stealthily, Robert produced an unintended noise with each movement. At first, he expected his racket to reveal his presence to his prey. After a few failed attempts at silence, he realized no matter how many sticks cracked under his weight or how many piles of dead leaves he crunched, the two gleefully fleeing females did not hear him. They were so noisy, he didn't even have to keep them in sight. They made no attempt to cover their trail, and not once did they look over their shoulders. They were so ridiculously unguarded, he was assured of success. Their lack of wariness made the prey even more alluring to the predator. He was thoroughly enjoying stalking them through the woods.

Ah, yes. His rewards would be great.

\*\*\*

## Chapter 20: The Reunion

"British soldiers!" cried Cordelia.

"Where?" Will's head whipped around as the rest of the foraging party drew to attention.

"There, on that old log. Next to Trio's feet. That will produce a fine dye for Mistress Nelly's wool."

"Oh, I thought you meant people," laughed Will, relief filling him. After all, the safety of the foraging party fell to him today.

"What color will it make?" asked Dale as he gently pushed Trio out of the way so he could gather the red-topped lichen.

"Pink to maroon. Do not mix it in with the fiddleheads. We do not to want to be eating it accidently."

"We should train Trio to find the plants we want," said Will. "They use pigs to find truffles. Why not use—"

Trio soft growl interrupted him. The small dog stood at attention, his entire body quivering and alert, the intensity of his growls increasing. Will signaled the other foragers. Immediately, everyone silently melted into the nearest bush. To any casual observer, the growling dog was by himself.

Will unsuccessfully scoured the woods for the source of Trio's alarm. What if it was the sheriff's men? Soldiers had never gotten close to the camp before. Had he allowed the foraging party to drift too far from camp? He had to find a way to protect them.

Suddenly, he understood his mother's sacrifice. She had protected both Scottie and the camp by allowing herself to be taken. All this time, he had been so angry with her decision to reveal herself when she could have avoided capture by remaining hidden. He had believed her choice to be one of bad judgment, but it was clear there had not been a choice at all, just as he had none now. He had to draw any threat away from his young friends.

Yes, now he understood his mother's sacrifice.

He quickly ascertained where the others were hidden. Dale would be able to lead them to safety. Perhaps Will could lead the threat away and still avoid capture. He was a lot faster than his mother. But if he was to be taken so they could escape, so be it. Heart thudding, he selected a bush set away from the younger foragers. Certain they had not yet been discovered, he darted for it.

"Will!" whispered Dale. "What are you doing?"

Will put a cautionary finger to his lips and shrugged regretfully at his friend. Dale scowled but signaled his understanding. There was no turning back now.

Will prepared to dash to another shrub, but froze. Over Trio's growling, he could hear the sounds of running footfalls from behind the hill.

*** *** ***

"Whew! I am not as young as I used to be!" Mistress Jocelyn said breathlessly as she crested the hill. Staggering to a tree, she leaned one hand against it and rested the other on her hip.

"Anyone would have difficulty running in those skirts," encouraged Rianne. "Be not of faint heart. We are nearly there." She was going to have to save people more often. This was much more fun than hunting.

"Mother!"

They both turned at the sound of Will's joyful greeting. With a happy cry, Mistress Jocelyn plunged down the hill toward her son. He met her halfway, locking her in an embrace that knocked the wind out of her.

"Oh, my darling boy!" Her words were thick with emotion.

Pleased to witness the reunion, Rianne watched them from the top of the hill, scanning the area for the others. "Nice job, lads. I can see nary a one of you," she called as she picked her way down the hill.

"Then how do you know they are here?" Mistress Jocelyn linked arms with Will and joined Rianne in her descent.

Will answered for Rianne. "We are no longer allowed to leave the camp unless we are in a group for safety."

The cheerful heads of the foraging party popped out of an assortment of greenery, all smiling, that is, save one.

"Something is wrong, m'lady," said Cordelia. She approached the still growling Trio, whose hackles were now raised. He took a step in the direction from which Rianne had just come.

"Mother, were you followed?" Will put a protective arm around her waist and ushered her forward.

"I do not know," she said, alarm on her face.

Rianne was not going to take any chances. "Quickly! Groups of two," she whispered as she unslung her bow. "Return to camp in a roundabout manner. Stay alert. Stay safe. I shall check—"

Suddenly, with an eruption of barks, Trio charged the hill.

"Trio!" cried Cordelia, giving chase to the rapidly disappearing dog.

"Cordelia, come back!" Dale shoved his sack at another boy and charged up the hill after her.

"Dale! No!" Rianne's command stopped his pursuit. "You must make sure everyone reaches safety. I shall fetch Cordelia. The rest of you, *go*. Now!"

Rianne sprinted back up the hill, shifting her bow and reaching for an arrow as she ran.

\*\*\*

## Chapter 21: Trauma to Trio

"What the f—" Robert unsuccessfully scrambled away from the snapping jaws of a little three-legged dog that had appeared out of nowhere. It managed to get hold of his pant leg and was holding on for dear life, growling as they struggled. Tripping over something, Robert fell backward.

*For Chrissakes!* The mutt didn't even come up to his knee. Robert tried kicking it off with his free foot. When that didn't work, he started feeling around on the ground for a weapon. His hand closed around a hefty branch. Snatching it up, he wielded it like a club, catching the small assailant in the ribs. It yelped, losing its grip.

"Yeah! Take *that*, Cujo." Robert jumped to his feet in case the mini attack dog went at it again. "Where the hell did you come from? I'll bet you belong to the outlaws."

If so, it meant someone could be almost upon him. He had to get out of there or risk capture. His hopes for finding the outlaw camp had just gone *poof* because of an overzealous mutt. Frustrated, he walked over to the dog, who was lying on the ground, still growling.

"This is your fault, you stupid little…" Robert drew back his leg and kicked the dog. Trio yelped and was silent.

"Serves you right," he muttered.

Robert looked over his shoulder toward the sounds of someone running his way. He could not be humiliated by capture. Without a backward glance, he took off, not slowing until he neared the fair. Wiping the sweat from his brow, he peeled his tunic away from his chest to allow in cooler air. The clothes of a noble were not exactly made for a summer run.

Regaining his composure, he strutted into the fair, consoled with the knowledge he was the only one who knew of his failed attempt to locate the outlaws' camp. However, there was still time. He now knew the general direction of the camp and would be paying another visit to the forest very soon.

Meanwhile, the redhead might still be waiting for him at the jousting tournament. He smoothed his hair and straightened his tunic. He might yet be able to salvage the day.

***

Rianne found Cordelia crying as she knelt next to an unresponsive Trio. She looked up at Rianne's approach.

"He kicked him," Cordelia sobbed.

Rianne scrutinized the forest around them, but whoever had done this was gone. She knelt beside the grieving girl. "Perhaps Trio attacked him, and he had no other choice," she said as she ran her hands over the dog's body. Trio's tail thumped weakly in the leaves.

"Trio?" whispered Cordelia.

"Cord, I am only trained in the care of people, not dogs. We must get him back to camp."

"We can use my bag to carry him." Disregarding the plants she had collected, she helped Rianne gently lay Trio on it.

Wrapping the edges of the bag around him, Rianne shouldered her bow and lifted the dog, trying not to disturb his injuries. Trio whined softly but did not struggle. As Rianne hoisted him closer to her shoulder, he licked her cheek.

"That is a good sign, is it not?" asked Cordelia.

Unsure, Rianne replied, "I am sure it is." She started walking. "Keep your wits about you, Cord. We do not want to be responsible for betraying the camp."

Cordelia scrutinized the area. "I hope he follows us. I shall kick him like he kicked Trio!"

"Cord, was Trio attacking him?"

"Yes, but he would never hurt a good person. Dogs know people. Trio would only attack a bad man."

"Has he ever attacked anyone before?"

"Just the man who broke into our house last year." Cord shuddered at the memory. "*He* was definitely bad."

"Well, good or bad, if the man was being attacked, it would be only natural he would kick back to protect himself."

"Aye, miss, but he hit Trio with a branch first. Trio did not get up after. The knave kicked him while he was down. I saw him from behind a tree." Cordelia's eyes brimmed with tears. "Who would kick a three-legged dog, miss?"

*Who would kick a three-legged dog, indeed?* She had no answer.

Cordelia scanned the woods behind them. "The next time I go to the fair, I am going to find that black-hearted knave."

"What do you mean, 'the next time'?" asked Rianne, stopping to stare at the younger girl. "Cordelia, have you been sneaking into the fair?"

"We all have, miss. The guards do not pay us any heed. They only look for our parents. They do not recognize children. Why, I have walked by the sheriff himself and said 'good day'."

Rianne closed her hanging mouth and resumed walking. "Unbelievable."

Cord checked behind them for trouble. "When I find out who he is…."

***

## Chapter 22: Things Appear Different by Moonlight

"Quietly, sir. We do not want to disturb the dog." Gil held the tent flap for Petir as he entered his new home.

"Now that Mistress Jocelyn has been rescued by Maid Rianne, I guess you're stuck with me," said Petir as he hobbled in. "Do you take care of all the camp's injured?"

"Purely coincidence. Cordelia's mother refused to allow the dog in their tent until she is sure he will survive. I believe Victoria sincere in wanting to ease Cordelia's distress, but I also think ultimately Victoria will use Trio as leverage for getting her daughter into a dress."

"Good luck with that," snorted Petir. "Missy Cordelia is as stubborn as Missy Rianne."

Gil chuckled as he secured the tent flap. He walked over to Petir and held up a knife.

"What's this?"

"Your first lesson in wood carving. There was an old wood carver named Phillip Fagans who said there were two types of carvers; those who carve to aid their thought, and those who thought to aid their carving."

Intrigued, he accepted the knife. "Which one are you?"

"I be a bit of both, when it suits me. What about you, young sir?"

"Me? That's easy. I'm going to need all the aid I can get for my carving."

Gil grinned. "What would you like to make?"

"I don't know. Maybe one of those wooden flutes everyone has. Hey, wait. How about an arrow for Maid Rianne?"

"Both are ambitious for a beginner. Why don't you begin with a small bowl and work your way up?"

"A bowl?" It sounded like another summer camp ashtray was about to be created. "Sure. Why not?"

Gil chuckled at his impatience. "Ah, young sir, you must learn to—"

"Walk before you run. I get it. Okay, where do we start?"

Gil showed him how to hold the knife. After being instructed how to envision his end product, Petir settled onto a pallet of blankets with a piece of wood for practice. Across from him, his three-legged tent-mate shifted in his sleep.

*Who would kick a three-legged dog while it was down?*

Inspiration struck. *I'm going to make Trio a water dish.*

Positioning the knife in his hand, he cautiously stroked the wood. This wasn't so hard. He resumed more enthusiastically and was soon lost in his work.

After a while, Petir's body began to protest his awkward position on the pallet. He gingerly inspected his hamstring as he stretched his back. It sure was healing quickly. He'd be able to give up the crutch soon. That should make it easier to keep up with Rianne.

*Will you listen to yourself? You can't make any plans. This isn't real. At any moment, this entire world could disappear. For all you know, you have already seen her for the last time.*

Surprisingly, a wave of melancholy swept through him, a ridiculously inappropriate wave of melancholy. First of all, this was a dream. Second of all, Rianne lived a life he only visited in computer games. His world and hers could never blend.

Or could it? Petir took off his shirt, blew out the light, and lay down, stretching his aching body. He folded his hands under his head and stared at the top of the tent, trying to picture Maid Rianne in his world. She'd be in high school, probably a senior. What about…

*Maid Rianne, in jeans, playing video games?* Sure. Give her a week, and she'd be the top scorer.

*Archer Rianne playing high school sports?* Actually, it wasn't too hard to picture her, hair tied back in a ponytail, spiking a volleyball.

*Warrior Rianne getting her cute little butt whipped at Ping-Pong?* He grinned. After all, he was the reigning tournament champ. He could smoke her easy. Then, he'd give her lessons. He'd have to wrap his arms around her to show her how to hold the paddle, and who knows where that could lead? To a date, maybe?

*Maid Rianne on a date?* Petir's gut hollowed reflexively with the certainty Rianne, in his world, would be dating someone else. Someone who was heroic. And strong. *And don't forget handsome.* He'd probably be like…Thor.

*Yeah, Thor would be perfect for her. Not a Ping-Pong paddle wielding, computer jockeying, class-A nerd like me.*

His distressing thoughts drove him out of bed. He grabbed his shirt and tried to quietly slip out without disturbing his tent-mates. As he lifted the flap, moonlight splashed on the man and dog. Trio was still asleep, now snuggled in the crook of Gil's arm. Gil watched Petir go, raising a questioning eyebrow. Petir shrugged helplessly at the unspoken question, bowed his head, and sadly limped into the moonlight.

\*\*\*

Rianne nervously bit her lip as she headed for Lord Petir's tent. What was she doing? Her mind must be truly addled. She should not feel nervous.

*He is of no consequence to me other than as my patient. My only concern is for his injury. I am his healer and nothing more. I have everything I need in Lord Robert. He is handsome. And smart. And he never shies away from competition, or any type of challenge. I am so lucky—*

She stopped short at the unexpected sight of Lord Petir standing outside his tent, studying a cloth he held. His shirtless physique was more slender than that of Lord Robert's rugged build, but Lord Petir was solidly built and, admittedly, quite attractive.

*Things certainly appear different by moonlight*, she thought uneasily.

Lord Petir sighed and shook the cloth, revealing it to be his shirt. He donned it and stood staring at the moon peeking between the trees. He looked so very sad; her heart went out to him.

He must be missing someone. Rianne worried her lip with her teeth. Surely Lord Petir had an intended. He was so clever and funny; he appeared to be curious about everything. Mistress Nelly told her he had tried his hand at spinning wool. Little Scottie had described Lord Petir's attempts with the bellows. She herself had observed his witless efforts when he challenged Cordelia with the staff. Lord Petir spoke to everyone, no matter their age or station. He was friendly and confident and … and, until now, never seemed discouraged.

*He certainly did not kiss me like he has an intended.*

Lord Petir sighed once again and shifted his gaze, suddenly locking onto Rianne. His startled expression instantly transformed to a pleased, almost tender smile.

Rianne felt a flush rise in her cheeks. *Thank goodness it be dark. He might misconstrue.* "Lord Petir." She sounded breathless to her own ears. What must he think? She tried again. This time her voice was strong and purposeful, as well it should be. "Lord Petir, I have come to treat your injury, if you are willing."

"Willing? I'll say I'm willing!" All of his sadness evaporated. "Wait. You don't want to do it in my tent, do you? It's full up."

Rianne smiled. "No, not your tent. I do not want to disturb the others. I have a cloth upon which you can lie. We can work by the campfire."

Lord Petir bobbed his head enthusiastically. "Sounds good to me. I, uh, left my crutch in the tent. Mind if I lean on you?"

Rianne was not fooled by his exceedingly innocent expression. She was fairly certain he would not attempt another transgression after she had so definitively refused him, but should he choose to act the knave, she was ready for him. There were still some people talking at the fireside. That should forestall any problems.

*There shall be no further indiscretion,* she firmly reminded herself.

Rianne realized he still awaited her reply. "Certainly, m'lord. You may lean on me."

She felt slightly alarmed at the prospect of his proximity but, at the same time, slightly aflutter. Suppressing the latter, she shifted the cloth to one side and slid her arm around his waist. His arm settled comfortably across her shoulders. She fit into its crook perfectly.

"Here, let me carry that." Lord Petir plucked the cloth from her and threw it over his other shoulder.

*You are far too pleased with his chivalry, Rianne. And far too comfortable with his arm around you.*

They slowly made their way to the campfire, guided by moonlight and firelight. He stumbled once. His sharp intake of air confirmed what she needed to know; his injury was real. She tightened the arm threaded around his waist. He responded by drawing her closer. This was dangerous ground. She needed to take control of the situation.

"We do not want you to trip in the dark, m'lord. You could worsen your injury."

"My thoughts exactly." His voice betrayed a grin obscured by the night. "I'm not holding you too tight, am I? I can support more of my weight if you can't handle it."

"Oh, I can handle it."

The soft voices murmuring near the crackling flames drifted toward them. Fryer stood up to add another log to the fire, then returned to re-drape his arm across his wife's shoulders. She sighed and leaned into him. Gypsy Ana and Mistress Aileen were in deep conversation but paused to softly greet the newcomers. Feeling very self-conscious, Rianne wiggled out from under Lord Petir's arm. Somehow it felt too intimate in front of these people.

"I am about to tend to Lord Petir's injury," she said as if an explanation was required. She spread out the cloth. Her patient limped over to it and sat down. She settled by his side and realized she did not know where to start. The short pants he wore made for easy access to the back of his leg, but she found his gaze unnerving.

"'Twould be better if he were on his stomach," advised the head healer.

Much to Rianne's relief, Lord Petir flipped over. Removing a flask of oil from her pocket, she proceeded. Her long, slow strokes increased warmth and circulation in preparation for honing in on the specific injury. He sighed contentedly.

*He has nice legs.*

That was not a proper thought for a healer. Rianne needed distraction from Lord Petir immediately. She focused her attention on the fire-lit conversations around them.

"Will you be staying the night, then?" asked Mistress Aileen.

"Nay, I shall be heading back soon," replied the old Gypsy.

"In the dark?" Fryer Tuck's voice had a disapproving sharpness to it. "Nay, not without an escort."

"Are you offering to accompany me, sir?" teased Gypsy Ana. "And what if you are taken prisoner?"

"If you, in your bright skirts, can slip back and forth so easily, I am sure I can make it back safely under the cover of night." Fryer Tuck's usually cheery brogue was tinged with stubbornness.

Gypsy Ana gave him a look of affection. "Nay, I shall not risk depriving your wife of your company, sir, nor the camp of your fine cooking."

"You will if you insist on returning to the village tonight," responded Fryer Tuck.

"Why not stay with me in the healer's tent," suggested Mistress Aileen. "We can continue our conversation there."

The elderly Gypsy smiled warmly at the company around the dying campfire. "Thank you for your kindness," she acquiesced.

"A blessing upon you all. It appears, my dear Aileen, you are to have a guest tonight."

"It is settled, then." Fryer stood up and stretched. "What say ye, wife?"

"Oh, my!" She was trying in vain to hide a yawn. "Fryer, please put another log on the fire for the young people." She also stood and stretched. "Good evening, one and all."

"Let us also take leave of this fine company," said Mistress Aileen. She stood and extended her hand to her elderly companion.

And just like that, once again, Rianne found herself alone with Lord Petir.

This was not good.

\*\*\*

## Chapter 23: Alone at Last

This was great. They were finally alone. Petir was fairly certain his dream was starting to pick up again. He had gone from thinking he might never see Maid Rianne again to a massage next to a campfire. Firelight. Moonlight. Chirpy night noises. He could not have planned it better.

*Let the indiscretions begin!*

Maid Rianne's hands were no longer moving.

"What's the matter?" he asked, propping himself so he could see her.

"Oh. Nothing is wrong. I merely noticed the others have all left, and ...."

*Oh, yeah. The dream is definitely about to pick up. Let's help this along.* "Did you want to save the massage for a later time? I'm sure my leg will be fine if you do."

"Oh, no, sir. It is my duty to help you get well as quickly as possible. I shall continue."

Disappointed, Petir emitted a noncommittal "Fine," and flopped back down on the blanket.

He had to admit the massage felt great. With his eyes closed, it was easy to imagine her touch as being affectionate. *Yeah, indiscretions can wait until the massage is done.*

Amazing how much detail came with this dream. He could smell the campfire, hear the crackling flames, feel its heat along one side of his body. In the background, he could hear the night noises combo. An occasional breeze pushed aside the smell of the fire, replacing it with a summer nighttime smell of earth, ferns, and leaves. Then there were the goose bumps Maid Rianne was generating. *I wonder if she can feel them on my legs.*

The thought made him feel self-conscious. Hopefully, she would just think he was cold.

\*\*\*

As Rianne worked, she listened to the frogs peeping in the woods and watched the fireflies sporadically flashing their signal for a mate. She caught herself watching the firelight play across Lord Petir's hair. He was lying with his chin propped on his fists.

"Hey! Fireflies!" His delight was endearing. "I haven't seen fireflies in years."

"Aye. It seems the older we get, the less time we spend outside," murmured Rianne.

"Ain't that the truth? That's why I started geodashing. It gave me a chance to get out and do some exploring."

"Geodashing, m'lord?" Rianne was unfamiliar with the term.

"Oh, never mind. It's not important," he sighed.

She felt a flash of irritation. That was exactly what Lord Robert did when she inquired about his time away from her. And here she was, thinking the two were so different.

Rianne added her own sigh. *Perhaps it is universal male behavior.*

"But I sure met more people than I expected." She could hear the humor in his voice.

"And more outlaws," she responded in kind.

"Hey," Lord Petir propped himself up on his elbows so he could see her. "If you don't mind me asking, how did you all come to be here?"

"In a camp full of outlaws? I do not know all of their stories, although I imagine the elders do. Some became fugitives by choice. Some came because there was no honorable alternative."

"But how did *you* come to be here?"

"Myself, I wanted to side with the weak and the brave, to have a chance to put my skills to use for something other than merely hitting a target."

"Huh." Lord Petir resumed his prone position cradling his head on his fists. "Well, you're great with targets. I checked out your handiwork in the practice arena. You're good. I mean, you are *really* good!"

Rianne felt flushed at his uncensored praise. He actually admired her pursuits, the same pursuits Lord Robert deemed inappropriate and unbecoming in a lady.

"Some believe my desire to be an archer unmaidenly," she confessed.

"Unmaidenly? Are you kidding me? *Unmaidenly*? I think it's so hot."

"Hot, m'lord?" Had she heard right?

"Yeah, you know…on fire, smoking, crazy, cool…." Lord Petir paused as if weighing his words, then sighed impatiently. "Oh, what the hell. I might as well just say it."

He propped himself up on his elbow again and twisted to see her. "The reason you are so damn hot, with your bow and your staff and whatever else you carry in your arsenal, is because you are so confident. You strut around here like you are some kind of champion."

"I do not strut." A wave of embarrassment washed over her.

"Well, then, you should because you got it going on."

"Your words confuse me, m'lord, but I do know you should not speak so."

"Why not? Things could change overnight. I might never see you again. This is a dream world, a fantasy, so I got nothing to lose."

Lord Petir changed to a sitting position and wrapped his arms around his knees. "Maid Rianne, you are the most incredible girl I have ever known. I wish I had one tenth of your confidence."

An energetic warmth rushed into Rianne's very core, heating her face and warming her heart.

"You, Lord Petir? Why, you exude bravado and audacity. You approach complete strangers and leave them feeling like they are old friends. You even pay attention to the children. If I may share this in confidence, sir, there had been talk amongst the elders about trading you for Mistress Jocelyn, but you won their hearts almost immediately. Even William the Blacksmith voted against sending you away."

"Wow. That would've sucked. The only reason I like being in this…this realm is because of you."

"How can you say you lack confidence when you address me thusly?"

"Believe me, this is not typical. Don't get me wrong. I'm plenty confident about the things I'm good at, but I'm not good at everything. Trust me on that."

"Such as using weapons?" Rianne gave Lord Petir a sassy grin.

"Exactly! But I am confident I can learn." He responded in kind.

"Actually, m'lord, you picked up the staff unusually quickly. Why do you think that is?"

Lord Petir leaned in closer to her, making her insides flutter. "Maybe it's because you are such a great teacher."

He leaned even closer, and her insides began to jump. "Do you think you could drop the 'Lord' and just call me Petir tonight?"

Without further warning, he gently kissed her cheek.

"Thank you, Rianne." He leaned back, apparently oblivious to the confusion he had created in her. "Of course, it could be due to my being a Ping-Pong champ. Lightning reflexes and all."

"Ping-Pong, m'l—Petir?"

He waved his hand dismissively. "Forget it. They don't have it around here. Not important. Anyway, on the coolness scale, it certainly doesn't rate up there with pummeling a bad guy with a staff." He laughed shortly. "Not that swinging a staff would fit anywhere in my world anyway."

"Sometimes," murmured Rianne, "I feel like *I* do not fit into my world.

"Really?" Petir looked surprised. "I feel the same way."

He looked at her for a moment then reached out and drew her closer to him.

*What is he going to do?* Rianne's heart began thumping. *What am I going to do?*

Surprisingly, he shifted both of their positions so they were seated side by side. He reached around them, pulled up the cloth on which he had been lying, and firmly wrapped it around both of their shoulders. He settled back to watch the burning embers. Rianne relaxed against him, warmed by the affectionate intimacy of the gesture.

Lord Petir had just unknowingly committed the biggest indiscretion of all. He had touched her heart.

## Chapter 24: Crunch Time

Hours later, Fryer Tuck found them in the same position, still talking quietly, staring at the dying embers. Self-conscious, Rianne leaned away from Lord Petir.

"Me Molly sent me to fetch ye, Maid Rianne," Fryer Tuck said softly. "Off with you now. The sun will be up shortly."

He turned to Lord Petir. "Do you need any help to your tent, your lordship?"

"No thanks. Just a hand up will do."

Fryer grasped their extended hands and hauled them both to their feet. Lord Petir groaned, most likely with the same stiffness she herself was feeling. Fryer stepped away to the pit on the pretense of stirring the remains of an expiring fire.

After gingerly stretching her own cramped muscles for a moment, she turned to find Lord Petir enigmatically studying her. Somehow, sitting shoulder to shoulder, staring at the dying fire had released a dialogue between them, candid and honest. After an evening of exchanging thoughts without exchanging glances, she felt awkward meeting his eyes.

She busied herself with shaking and folding the cloth that had shielded them from the cool summer night's breeze. Pausing before taking her leave, she gathered her courage, raised her head, and boldly met his gaze. Fully aware Fryer Tuck was trying unobtrusively to eavesdrop, she softly shared, "For me, this night doth end too soon. Good evening, m'lord."

*** 

Petir watched Rianne walk away, bemused because somehow he felt like she had just kissed him. *You are so lame.* Ignoring the irony of his thoughts, he carefully limped his way through the dark toward his tent, mentally chastising himself as he went.

*What just happened? Were you, or were you not, in the middle of the world's greatest seduction scene? Moonlight...firelight...beautiful girl...*

*And what did you do when it came down to crunch time?*

*You...you* snuggled*! Men everywhere will hang their heads in disgust.*

He waggled his head in confusion. What had gone wrong? He had already made it to first base with Maid Rianne. Snuggling was like being kicked out of the batter's box. It certainly wasn't the second base he had been minimally expecting.

"So explain one thing to me, Petir Capota," he said to himself. "Why do you want to do it again?"

He lay awake for a long time after returning to his tent. He was worse off than when he first stepped out. Sooner or later, he was going to wake up from this dream, and reality would resume. Rianne would remain a wispy figment of his imagination, as would the incredible night they had just spent together. The inevitability of losing her felt ten times worse. Afraid to fall asleep, he drifted off, muttering a prayer.

"Please let me wake up here tomorrow. Please give me one more day with Rianne. Please...."

## Chapter 25: Another Day in Dreamland

*Yes! Yes! Yes! Yes!*

Petir was opening his eyes to yet another morning in the outlaw camp. Gil was up and gone, but Trio had somehow found his way over to his side. Trio's tail thumped. Petir petted the dog as he replayed the events from last night. He tried to enjoy lying there, thinking about Rianne by the campfire, but something didn't feel right. Uneasy, he finally sat up.

*Weird. Dreams aren't supposed to run this long, are they?*

But what else could it be? *Time travel, maybe?*

*Hah.*

Maybe he had severely injured himself when he fell out of the tree, and his subconscious was making all this up. Unfortunately, that was a more probable option than time travel. Brain damage, maybe? He shivered in the coolness of early morning.

At least there was a silver lining. If it was brain trauma, his mind was doing a damn good job of creating this realm. He shivered again. A great dream wasn't enough silver in the lining to compensate for a prospect that frightening.

*Nah, this has to be a dream.* He was going with the less scary alternative. *I'm not that surprised anymore to find myself here each morning. I'm fairly certain that means something. I'll probably be waking up soon.* He calmed himself with the thought.

Too bad. This was a most excellent dream.

He stretched his shoulders, made sore from trying to master the staff. And too bad he'd never get to use his newly acquired skills, so highly prized in Maid Rianne's world. It wasn't just the combat techniques. Where was he going to apply his new knowledge about spinning wool. Or making plant dyes. Or smelting metals?

*Nowhere, that's where.*

Anyway, all that info was probably just made up in his head. *Who eats milk thistle and ferns?* Petir had had dreams where he could speak a foreign language, but, of course, could not when he awoke. When this dream finished, he probably would remember just as little. He wilted a little under the weight of his thoughts, then straightened.

*No way am I going to forget Rianne.* Petir felt almost reverent as he brought her to mind. She embodied living life to its fullest, facing and surmounting challenges, and living outside the hand fate dealt you. She was—

Alight with excitement, Dale's face popped through the tent flap. "Come quick-like. They bring a prisoner," he said in a hushed tone. "Make no noise. If it be a trap, we will need to flee."

"What? Flee from a prisoner?" Petir scrambled to his feet.

"No, no. If he leads the sheriff's soldiers to us, we must be ready. Our hunting party has gone out to see if he has been followed." Dale handed him his crutch and prepared to leave. "Don't worry, m'lord, I shall return for you. I can bring you to a safe hiding place."

"No way. I'll be too slow." He bent to scoop up Trio. "You go where the others tell you to go. I'll be fine."

"Cordelia will never forgive me if I abandon you." Dale blushed through his defiant grin. "Besides, you have her dog."

## Chapter 26: A Message from the King

"What is yon commotion?" Fryer Tuck asked in a hushed tone as Petir emerged from the tent.

"A messenger! A messenger from the king himself!" James Potter softly called as he ran by.

Fryer and Petir watched as a blindfolded youth stumbled but was set upon his feet by the two larger men guiding him.

"Remove the blindfold," suggested a young teenage girl. "Let us get a good gander at him!" She giggled.

"Nay, lassie. The less known, the better," advised Fryer.

"Aye, 'e shall be none the wiser. Who knows when we may be called upon to hide away in the future?" Turning toward the messenger, William growled, "What is your name, boy, and who sent you?"

The youth drew himself to full height and answered. "I be David Doncaster, and I have been sent by no one but the King himself."

"King Richard, the Lionheart?"

"Aye, there is no other. I bear his token, and a grand message at that!"

"Well, go on, lad. What tidings do you bring?"

"Amnesty has been granted for all those oppressed by the tyrannical rule of Prince John and who have yet remained loyal and faithful to our good King Richard, the Lionheart."

"Is it a trick?" called someone from the crowd.

"He has not been followed," called a breathless hunter, trotting from the woods.

"Nay, 'tis no trick," the messenger said earnestly. "On Saturday next, there is to be a celebration like no other, a celebration in honor of the return of our good King Richard. Pardons written in the king's own hand will be dispensed to all who stood against the usurper, Prince John."

Petir watched as mixed emotions flitted across the faces of the camp folk. Finally, William Smythe roared, "I hope King Richard's writing arm is as strong as his sword arm. There be fifty-nine pardons in need of writing!"

The camp broke into a raucous cheer.

Mistress Jocelyn found her way to William's side, and he enveloped her in a hug. "Would you do it again, Jocie?" he asked tenderly.

"How can you ask that, you wretched outlaw?" She smiled at him.

"Ah, but outlaw no longer."

She giggled as he swung her around. He set her down gently and hugged her to him. They both gazed around at the grounds that had sheltered them. He sighed. "I shall miss this place, Jocie."

"Time to move back to proper society, my dear." She gazed at him with love and murmured, "Aye, I would do it again."

"I told you this wouldna last forever." Petir hadn't noticed Mistress Molly standing there until she spoke.

"Nothing good ever does," said Petir, thinking about Maid Rianne in the moonlight. "Where will you go?" *Where will Maid Rianne go?*

*Where will I go?*

"We shall see what has become of our farm in Coventry."

"Coventry? Is there a Coventry in England, too?"

"Of course there is."

*Huh. A Coventry in England* and *a Coventry in Connecticut?* A thread of reality was trying to weave itself into his dream-babble.

Fryer stood back with arms folded across his chest and a wistful look on his face. "Aye, this is the life. I do not relish returning to the life of a common laborer after living carefree as an outlaw."

"Nor I." Gil walked up and slapped Fryer on the back. "We are gathering everyone together for a council meeting."

"Where will Maid Rianne go?" Petir asked Fryer as they joined the others walking toward the meeting place.

"That unfortunate creature will be returned to her loved ones." He woefully wagged his head. "Maid Rianne thinks we do not know who she is, but we do. Such a waste is that."

"Her loved ones? You mean her parents?"

"Regrettably, no. She lost her parents in an accident when she was but a tiny thing. She will be returned to her guardian."

"Her guardian? What's he like?"

"She is the ward of a man called King by many. From what she says, he was coming to bear influence on the selection of Maid Rianne's betrothed." He leaned forward conspiratorially. "If you ask me, *that* is the reason she ran away to the forest."

Little John ran up, and Fryer Tuck swung him to his shoulders, preventing any further conversation. A genial commotion enveloped Petir. The messenger's blindfold was being removed by a group of giggling girls. Gil clapped two pieces of wood together to quiet the gathering crowd. But Petir barely noticed any of it, distracted by a growing sense of dread. Was Maid Rianne being forced into marriage?

"As you may have heard," announced Gil, "we have received word from King Richard. He promises pardons to all."

The camp erupted again into cheers and hugs.

Mistress Molly raised her hands for their attention. "We shall break camp two days hence. Take what you can carry and return for the rest. Leave separately and with stealth. Until you have in thy possession the king's seal, you may yet fall prey to that devil, the sheriff."

Order disintegrated as the crowd began discussing the news. Gil banged the two pieces of wood together to regain their attention.

"Who will volunteer to return later and tend to the site?" he asked. "Henceforth, it must appear as though none have been biding here. Who knows if fate will deem it necessary to call upon this place for protection again?"

Several of the men and boys raised their hands.

"So it is agreed," said Mistress Molly. "The womenfolk will tend to the babes, hearth, and home, and the menfolk will secure the camp after the grand event. Blessings be with thee."

"And with thee!" responded several.

*Oh, no.* Suddenly, everything was changing, and Petir was helpless to stop it. Panic set in.

*I guess it doesn't matter if I wake up soon or not.*

*No dream equals no Rianne.*

*Still dreaming equals no Rianne.*

Petir tried to calm himself. He had to find a way to prolong this until he could figure out an alternative.

This dream was beginning to suck.

## Chapter 27: Can Christopher Stay?

"Are you completely daft, Jonathan Allan Tuck?" Mistress Molly yelled as her youngest son stared intently at the ground. "How could you bring him here?"

Petir had just found Maid Rianne in the dispersing crowd of joyful outlaws when Mistress Molly's cry drew their attention to an unfamiliar little boy standing behind Little John.

"Lord Petir was allowed to remain," her son asserted. "And Christopher's family does not want him. All they do is fight. Please, Mother, let him stay. He will be happier with us."

"They shall never miss me." The new boy bowed his head sullenly. "And you cannot make me return," he added with slightly more bluster.

"*She* might not be able to make him return, but *I* certainly can," muttered Maid Rianne as she strode over to the little group.

However, the angry Mistress Molly was softening. She bent down toward Christopher, gesturing to Maid Rianne to wait.

"Christopher Lee, I know your parents are angry with each other," she said gently, "but they love you as much as I love Little John. Your mother will be beside herself until you return. You do know that, do you not?"

Christopher nodded reluctantly, head bowed.

"Then you must return, m'dear. There is no other way," Mistress Molly said, regarding the two forlorn little boys.

Little John put his arm around his friend's shoulders and tried again. "Could he not spend just the one night, Mother?"

"And have his own mother worry through the night? Come now, Little John," Mistress Molly admonished gently.

"We could send a message, Mother," he said excitedly. "Then she would not worry."

"Little John, you know it is not yet safe for us to travel. Who could carry a message to the fair without placing the entire camp in danger?"

"I could," said Maid Rianne stepping forward.

"A maid in men's clothing? You would be spotted instantly," said Mistress Molly dismissively.

"Aye, lass, clad in Nottingham green, she would," agreed Fryer Tuck as he walked up behind his wife. "But not clad as a maid ought to be. With the proper clothing, she would blend well with the other lassies attending the tournament."

Maid Rianne glared as Fryer Tuck beamed back at her triumphantly.

"I agree." Abruptly, she spun on her heel and headed for the maidens' tent she shared with the giggling teens. Petir watched her back stiffen as Fryer Tuck let out a shout of laughter.

Petir hobbled over to Mistress Molly as she smacked her husband on the arm. Skipping out of harm's way, Fryer Tuck continued to snicker as he headed back to his galley.

She turned to the boys. "*One* night."

With matching whoops of joy, the boys bounded off.

"I mean it! One night!" she called after them. "And only with permission!"

"Yes, Mother," Little John called over his shoulder.

"What was that all about?" Petir asked, staring at the tent housing the very angry Maid Rianne.

"Tradition," she supplied cheerfully. "Men do not appreciate change. My Fryer is a good man, but he does not approve of a *'lass in men's clothing. 'Tis simply not proper!'*" she said, imitating her husband's brogue.

"How dangerous is it for Maid Rianne to go to the fair?" Petir asked.

She pursed her lips, then answered in a light voice as she turned to go. "Well, now. That all depends on whether she is caught, now, does it not?"

Petir grabbed her arm. "Caught? What would happen if she got caught?"

"I… I imagine she would be questioned as to where our camp is located."

"And if she doesn't tell them?" Petir prodded.

"She would be taken to the sheriff."

"And then what?" snapped Petir. "Can you just tell me instead of playing 'Twenty Questions'?"

"Then all would be done for her. She would be returned to her betrothed, who has aligned himself with the sheriff," snapped Mistress Molly, shaking off his hand. "Are you satisfied?"

"Her *betrothed*?" said Petir, taken aback by both the news and the odd roiling in his stomach. Of course Maid Hottie had a boyfriend. He was an idiot to not have considered it before. She'd be scooped up immediately in any realm. "She is betrothed? To who?"

"Aye, to the blackest heart that ever walked. In a fortnight, none here will be able to lay claim to her."

*What the hell is a fortnight?* "What do you mean? Isn't she a little young?"

"He pressed her, and she gave her consent."

*Of course he pressed her. Any guy would be panting to make it permanent with Rianne.* "What…what's he like?"

"He be a fair evil man, a scoundrel named Robert Gisborne. Young Rianne believes him to be misguided in his judgment, but that knave is a consummate user of innocence. It was no accident he ended up on the right side of the sheriff. Foolish girl." Mistress Molly shook her head. "But there is no reasoning with her. She believes when this…" She waved vaguely at the camp. "…reaches its inevitable conclusion, all will be forgiven, and she will be content to return to the life she formerly led. Maid Rianne doesn't understand matters shall never be the same."

"Does…does she love him?" he asked as casually as he could.

Mistress Molly arched an eyebrow. "Not as much as you love her," she said with a knowing air.

"Me? Love Rianne? I don't love her. I just met her. How could I love her? She's a...a...a medieval maiden who...who wants to hit me with her staff whenever she gets pissed, for Chrissakes!" Petir gestured wildly with his free hand, barely noticing her steadying his crutch. "I'm a computer jockey who falls out of trees. We wouldn't last one day outside of this...this realm. Besides, a girl like that wouldn't go for a guy like me. She's Xena the Warrior Princess, and I'm...I'm ...I'm not even attracted to her," he ended unconvincingly, his face over-heated.

"'Tis most unfortunate, indeed." Mistress Molly lifted the hem of her skirts to leave. "That young maiden deserves a young man who would be a devoted lord and master, not a blackguard who corners any skirt, willing or not."

"What do you mean?" Petir limped after her as she headed back to her duties. "He cheats on her? Cheats on Maid Rianne?"

Shushing him, Mistress Molly glanced back.

Abashed, Petir peeked toward the maidens' tent and lowered his voice. "How could anyone cheat on someone like Maid Rianne?"

"Perhaps 'e is 'not even attracted to her.'"

"Not attracted to her? Not attracted to Maid Rianne?" he sputtered. "He'd have to be blind not to be attracted to—"

He paused as the flap to the maidens' tent lifted.

"Whoa!" breathed Petir.

Maid Rianne emerged from the tent clothed in an earth-brown dress befitting the times, rivaling anything twenty-first century Victoria's Secret had to offer. A white linen blouse was laced firmly into an embroidered bodice. The fabric hugged her slender frame, emphasizing the curves that had been distracting him for the last few days. Graceful swathes cascaded into a moving pool of cloth, gently swirling around her feet as she walked. The front of her dark hair had been swept up and somehow captured with lengths of yarn, but the rest of it tumbled down her back. Petir had never seen anything like it. She was perfect, except for the scowl on her reddened face.

"Not a word," Maid Rianne growled as she stormed past him. "Not a single word."

"I would take her advice, m'dear," Mistress Molly whispered. "And you might want to close your mouth before you trap yourself a fly."

Embarrassed, Petir snapped his mouth shut and hobbled after Maid Rianne.

*Her betrothed is cheating on that?*

\*\*\*

## Chapter 28: Off to the Fair

"Thou shalt not accompany me to the fair," Rianne repeated as she paused at the top of an embankment. The last thing she needed was Lord Petir following her like a puppy when she needed to find Lord Robert.

"Why not?" he huffed as he struggled up the hill, his crutch sliding in the leaves.

"I have no desire to be slowed down," she hedged.

He straightened up indignantly and immediately lost his balance. Staggering backward on the hillside, he was saved from tumbling by Rianne's firm grasp on his shirt. As she jerked him forward, he collided with her body. His free arm immediately wrapped around her waist for balance, pulling her close as they struggled to regain their equilibrium. Steady now, his embrace remained firm.

Even though Rianne stood higher on the hill, Lord Petir still looked down as he gazed into her eyes. Her pulse leapt. She watched as his green eyes darkened with an awareness that matched her own. Why was she fighting it? If she reached just a little bit, she would be able to taste his mouth again. It was so close, and the longer they stood there, the harder it was to resist the impulse. Was that her heart pounding so hard? Over an outlaw she had just met?

She tilted her head back the tiniest bit. He lowered his the tiniest bit. She sighed the smallest sigh and lightly tugged his shirt, guiding him toward her. She reveled in the warmth of his arm around her back.

And still they stood there.

Ignoring the angels of conscience perched on her shoulders, she leaned in, confirming the unspoken invitation. His breath was becoming as ragged as hers, but he did not close the gap between them. What was he waiting for? She rose on her toes, bringing her lips a hair's breadth from his. His sharp intake of air told her how much she was affecting him.

"You are betrothed?" he whispered.

"*What*?" Rianne cried, pushing away from him.

"Watch out!" Lord Petir shouted as he once more teetered.

Instinctively, Rianne grabbed for him again, this time inadvertently slamming his body into hers, propelling them backward. Trying to protect her from the fall, Lord Petir dropped his crutch as they toppled onto the hill. The leaves swirled around them with a gentle *swoosh* that accompanied Rianne's very unladylike "Oomph" as he landed on her.

Rianne's agitation bubbled to the surface and erupted. Lord Petir knew about Lord Robert? What was she doing? How was it he could recall Robert at a moment like this, but she had forgotten he even existed? How could she react this way when she belonged to another?

"To hell with it." Lord Petir lowered his head to kiss her.

"Wait," Rianne cried, effectively stopping him. "Who told you about—"

"Your betrothed?" supplied Lord Petir, raising his head, desire replaced by something else. "Word gets around," he said as he rolled off her.

Ignoring the sudden chill the absence of his body caused, she lay in the leaves next to him, silently watching the foliage tremble in front of a cloud-dotted sky. Although the sounds of their breathing were returning to normal, her thoughts and emotions remained in complete chaos.

Why did she feel so badly? Was it the guilty pleasure of the kisses they had shared or her inappropriate desire to experience it again? And with a stranger at that. Although she had heard many sought a harmless dalliance prior to a permanent commitment, this was not the proper behavior of someone with an intended.

Perhaps it was only due to their recent quarrel over her joining the outlaws.

*No, I must remain faithful to Lord Robert,* she sternly told herself. *I owe it to him not to dishonor him.*

"Lord Petir—" she began.

"Forget it!" he said brusquely. "I was out of line."

"Out of line?"

"Yeah. I shouldn't have kissed you yesterday." He sighed. "Or the first day." He sat up. "But in my defense, I thought you were coming on to me."

"Coming on to you?" Rianne sat up, indignant.

"Yeah, you know. Propositioning me? Encouraging me? You know, by the way you were…uh…touching me."

Rianne was incensed. "I am the healer! My touch was a healing touch!" she spat out, denying her own reaction to her massage.

"Healing touch, huh? Is that what you call it?" He snorted. "Well, *I* definitely felt better." He heaved himself to his feet and turned to look at her.

She could only imagine what her expression was portraying because he instantly became contrite.

"Well, I didn't know, okay?" he said defensively, reaching out to help her up.

Rianne considered ignoring his offered hand and scrambling to her feet on her own, but reality asserted itself. Only a fool would try to stand on a slope, slippery with leaves, in the tangled sea of her skirt. She ungraciously accepted his help, registering a tingle when his hand firmly closed around hers.

"Otherwise," he said as he braced himself to pull her up, "I *never* would have kissed you."

"Never?" She was pretty sure she had just been insulted.

He hauled Rianne to her feet. "Never in a million years."

"Ooh!" she cried, angrily snatching her hand from his. She stood for a moment, fists clenched at her sides, her outrage making her breathing quick and shallow. His eyes widened as she stomped past him to where his crutch had fallen. Snatching it out of the leaves, Rianne turned and leveled at his nose as if it was a sword. In her iciest voice, she said, "As I told you before, you will *not* accompany me to the fair. I have a message to deliver, *and a betrothed to find*, and I do not want you to hinder me."

She flung the crutch as hard as she could down the hill. Ignoring Lord Petir's protest, she gathered her skirts and ran lightly up the slope without a backward glance.

## Chapter 29: Too Many Lords

*What is* wrong *with you?* Rianne had no answer as she strode angrily through the forest. Accustomed to being in control of her emotions, she found this state of mind very confusing and extremely irritating.

*Lord Petir cannot compare to Lord Robert in any arena.* He was nothing more than an insolent cur, a momentary distraction. Lord Robert, so handsome and accomplished, was most decidedly the one for her. She had admired him from afar for too long. On the day he had first taken notice of her, he had completely swept her off her feet, and now she belonged to him. No other maiden could be so fortunate.

To her surprise, she was already approaching the fair and needed to take cover. Undoubtedly, the sheriff's men would be expecting a brash outlaw or two to try to sneak in. She needed to proceed with caution and focus. No more silly drivel in her head.

She paused, looked around, and positioned herself behind a tree. After scrutinizing the area, she headed for a closer bush.

She needed to see Lord Robert. That was all. Everything would be set right once they were together again. She simply had been too long without him. That was the source of her confusion.

*What are you going to tell him, Rianne?*

She had no idea.

Realizing she was standing out in the open, concealed by absolutely nothing, she sank to the ground behind the bush. She was going to get caught if she remained distracted by the thoughts competing in her head. She needed to think through this predicament. Better to do it now, rather than being preoccupied while stealing into the fair.

*If I was truly ready to commit to Lord Robert, I would not be distracted by a random ruffian like Lord Petir.*

It probably began because she was assigned to be his healer directly after quarreling with her intended. *It is easy to confuse a relationship between a healer and her charge as something more, but it still remains a mistake.*

Perhaps Lord Petir's pursuit of her was only because she was a female of appropriate age at the camp. *"Lord" indeed!*

But last night, in the moonlight, by the fire…. *I cannot deny it. Lord Petir touched my heart.*

How could she remain with one person when she was distracted so by another? There were too many lords in this picture.

*What am I going to say to Lord Robert? That I have been a silly girl?* She was not being fair to him. *He deserves someone as faithful as he is.* There was no question about it. She had to be honest with him and confess the situation.

*The conflict between the royals is resolved. Lord Petir will return to whence he came, and what will be left of my relationship with Lord Robert? He might choose to rescind his offer when he learns of my infidelity.* But that was a risk she would have to take. At least Rianne would know she had behaved nobly by being honest.

She crept forward. She needed to find Lord Robert before she lost her nerve.

## Chapter 30: An Easy Target

There he was, the perfect target and Rianne's ticket into the fair. She approached the elderly man fanning himself in the heat. He was very flushed and sweaty.

"Your pardon, sir." She curtsied gracefully in front on him. "Might I convince you to accompany me for some refreshment?"

He took in her apparel and nodded gratefully. "Yes, thank you. That is very kind of you, my dear. I do believe I have overdone it a bit."

As he leaned forward to stand, she took his arm and helped him. Arms linked, they slowly wound their way through the fair, chatting as they went. In her experience, no one looked twice at a maiden with an escort, especially an older gentleman who might be a relative. She located a shady place to sit and left him there while she fetched him a cool drink. She headed for the tavern run by Nora and Allan Lee, Christopher's parents.

"Some water, if you please, mistress," said Rianne to the florid woman behind the bar.

Mistress Nora handed over the requested water before recognizing Rianne's grin. Anxiously, the bartender looked around for trouble.

"You should not be here, my lady," Mistress Nora whispered. "The sheriff's men are everywhere."

"Aye, but I carry a message from your son," intoned Rianne.

"A message from my—" Mistress Nora grimly placed her hands on her hips. "He is not watching the jousting tournament with Little John, I take it?"

"No. He has run away to the forest to join our merry band," said Rianne. Checking for eavesdroppers, she delivered Christopher's note.

Mistress Nora unrolled it and laughed. "Prithee, Mother and Father," she read. "Allow us one night together in the forest. I will return forthwith on the morrow." She sighed and leaned on the bar with her head in her hands. "Well, at least he spelled everything correctly."

Rianne chuckled. "Mistress Molly will have him delivered forthwith *today* if that is your wish," she assured the irate mother.

"What was that boy thinking?" Mistress Nora responded in frustration.

"What news, fair Rianne?" Allan Lee came up behind her, carrying a tray of dirty dishes.

"Our son has abandoned us for the forest." Mistress Nora bleakly handed the note to her husband to read.

"The answer is yes," he said after a moment.

"Yes?" repeated Mistress Nora. "How can you say that? Do we know he will be safe?"

"Mistress Molly and Mistress Nellie are both there. There are children his age there. He will be well looked after."

Mistress Nora opened her mouth to protest, but he interrupted by taking her hands in his. "We need this night alone, wife. We need to smooth out our differences. You know he left because of our quarreling."

His wife reddened and glanced sideways at Rianne, who had judiciously stepped aside to let them hold their discussion in private.

"Barkeep!" called a customer.

"I shall tend to thee directly, sir!" answered Allan.

He turned back to his wife and quietly implored, "Say yes to him, and say yes to me, my love. We can fix this."

Mistress Nora leaned over the bar and kissed her husband, causing a raucous cheer to erupt from the crowded tables. Blushing, she conveyed her agreement to Rianne with wink.

After being waved off when she attempted to pay for her drink, Rianne left in search of her aged escort, feeling a lightness in her step which had been missing since she had left Lord Petir. She found the elderly man where she had left him, looking less florid after a few minutes in the shade. She handed him the water and sat with him while he drank. After making sure he connected with his family, she excused herself and bid him good day. She had one more stop to make before heading back to deliver the good news to the two little boys.

***

"Maid Rianne, what a pleasant surprise!" said Robert as he wheeled away from the wall upon which he had been leaning.

The last thing he had been expecting was for Rianne to show up after losing her in the forest yesterday. Commandeering her elbow, he quickly steered her away from the cute blond returning with their drinks. If he moved fast enough, he would not get caught. And, if he played his cards right, he could fix things with the blond later.

He guided Rianne quickly toward the tournament arena, a crafty plan forming in his mind. The sheriff was there with his guards, enjoying the joust. If Robert talked smoothly enough and walked quickly enough, he might be able to deliver Rianne right into their hands *and* make it look like an accident. They would take her prisoner. He would spend the night with the blond. Tomorrow, he would beg for Rianne's release, and who knew how a grateful Maid Rianne might repay him?

"Lord Robert, I must talk with you. Please, can we go someplace quiet?" asked Rianne as she tried to slow their pace.

"Yes, of course, my dear." He secured his grip on her arm, lost in his thoughts.

Rianne shrugged free and dug her heels in. "Lord Robert, what are you doing?"

He was at a loss. He was having difficulty adjusting from blond-trollop conversation to conversation befitting his intended, especially when he was busy plotting. What was she expecting? *Nice to see you in a dress for once?*

*Ah, I know what she wants.* He swept Rianne into an embrace and kissed her firmly. *Aye, that should do it.*

"Missed me, did you?" He grinned as she staggered back in surprise. "I've been thinking about you constantly, my love." He cradled her arm in his again and herded her once more toward the joust. "Where have you been? I have been so worried about you, what with the battling royals and all."

He continued to prattle, purposely letting the sound of his chatter crowd out any suspicious thoughts regarding his intentions that might arise in the mind of the unsuspecting maiden. This easy target was worth some money to him, and he was not about to lose her.

\*\*\*

## Chapter 31: Never Say Never

With the whereabouts of the fair remaining a mystery, Petir had no alternative but to find his way back to the camp. He found Gypsy Ana and Healer Aileen busily preparing herbs, which had been drying in the summer air since he had been there. They waved him over and handed him a mortar and pestle. After watching them grind dried plants for a few minutes, he sat down and imitated their motions.

"Maid Rianne is pissed at me," he confessed.

"What is 'pissed'?" asked the Gypsy.

Petir sighed. *They don't understand slang.* "She's mad at me."

"What did you do?" asked the healer.

"I kind of kissed her."

"What is 'kind of kissed her'?" asked the Gypsy.

*Stop using slang*, Petir reminded himself for the billionth time. "I definitely kissed her. How's that?"

"And she is angry because you kissed her?" asked the healer.

"I don't know." He stabbed the mortar with the pestle. "I think she's mad because I apologized for kissing her."

"Ahhh," the two women chorused.

"What?" He looked up, feeling completely clueless in the face of their certainty. "What is it? I was trying to be a gentleman."

"It depends. Why did you apologize?" Gypsy Ana was smirking at her friend.

"A guy like me should never kiss a girl like her. So I apologized."

"A girl like her? Because she has a betrothed?" asked the healer.

There was that word '*betrothed*' again. It had such an ugly ring to it. "Yes, if you really want to know. That's what I get for trying to be nice."

"Poor boy. It not only matters what you say. It matters how you say it," said Healer Aileen.

"Yes. What did you say? Exactly."

Petir felt warmed by more than the morning sun. "I said I was out of line, you know...inappropriate, and that I thought she was coming on to me...I mean, that she wanted to kiss me... and that, otherwise, I never would've kissed her."

The two women exchanged glances. The Gypsy appeared to have better control than the healer, who was trying to smother a giggle behind her palm.

"He said *never*," the healer managed to choke out.

"You said *never*?" the Gypsy said in a strangled voice.

"Actually, I said never in a million years."

The two women exploded in laughter.

"Idiot," gasped Gypsy Ana, wiping tears from her eyes.

"And 'e looks so intelligent, too," wheezed the healer.

"I'm glad you're both enjoying this so much." Petir was getting pissed. He could stand being laughed at by two little old ladies for only so long. What did they know anyway?

The healer snorted as she gasped for breath, which started up both women again.

"Real mature," muttered Petir, grinding the hell out of the innocent herbs.

"I need water." Gypsy Ana rose, fanning herself.

"I shall fetch it." Healer Aileen stood and patted Petir on the back. "Thank you. I have not laughed like that in a very long time."

"My pleasure." His sarcasm impacted her about as much as it impacted the herbs he was punishing.

"My dear boy." The Gypsy put her hands on his shoulders and gently jiggled him until he met her gaze. "Listen to your words. You told the girl, if it was your choice, you would not kiss her, *never in a million years*. Think!"

"Oh." Understanding blossomed. "Oh! But I meant it in a good way, you know, like being honorable."

"Is that the way she received it?"

"Nope," he said. "I thought she was going to hit me with my crutch."

Healer Aileen was returning with a dipper of water for her friend. She looked at Petir's face. "Ahh, so he understands now, eh?"

Petir pulverized the herbs in frustration. "I never should've kissed her in the first place."

This dream royally sucked.

\*\*\*

## Chapter 32: A Revealing Kiss

Something was not right. Actually, many things were not right. Rianne was finding herself closer and closer to the center of the fair when the cardinal rule was to remain on the perimeter for easy escape into the forest. She had allowed herself to be distracted by Lord Robert's snatched kiss. Her chaotic thoughts had shoved his strange behavior into the background. Rianne halted in her tracks. She needed to take command of the situation.

"What is it, Maid Rianne?" He was being unusually solicitous, behaving more like Lord Petir, who was almost always considerate of others.

He continued to tug at her elbow, but she needed to know something. She freed herself and turned to face him.

"Kiss me again," she said.

"What?"

"Kiss me again, please."

His expression turned smug. "Oh, so you liked that, did you?" He stepped closer and wrapped his arms around her waist.

Actually, she had not enjoyed the earlier kiss one bit. That is what had thrown her into turmoil. Rianne needed to know if it was because he had surprised her, or if….

"Just kiss me, please."

With a knowing chuckle, he lowered his head to hers and took possession of her lips. Rianne tried to conjure up the thrill this used to create, but nothing felt right. He lifted his head, revealing a self-satisfied smirk.

She looked at him, perplexed. *What am I doing with him?*

Lord Robert was egotistical, not lordly. *Have I always mistaken his arrogance for self-confidence?* The reason he did not indulge in kindness was not because he was driven to succeed. He simply was not kind. Rianne suddenly understood. He truly belonged with the sheriff.

*What is he doing with me?* Lord Robert had firmly draped his arm over her shoulder and was once again marching her though the crowd, blathering on about how much she was going to enjoy the joust.

She needed to know one more thing and again brought them to a halt.

"Lord Robert, how do you feel about me competing in the archery tournament tomorrow?"

"The archery tournament is tomorrow? I had forgotten." He nudged her into walking by his side and continued to steer her though the crowd. "I think you should do what makes you happy."

She beamed up at him. "I am so relieved. I would not want to displease you—"

Rianne tripped and was saved from falling by Lord Robert's firm embrace. She gasped as she clung to him.

"My ankle! I have twisted my ankle. How I hate these skirts." She winced as he helped her to a nearby bench.

"I cannot believe this," she moaned. "Now I shall not have a steady stance. I shall not be able to draw my bow." Tears filled her eyes as she bravely looked at Lord Robert. "Please, can you find me some ice to keep the swelling down?"

He stood there in frustration until her first tear ran down her cheek. He looked around. "You wait right here. Don't try to walk on it. You'll just make it worse. I shall return directly." Satisfied that she would comply, he headed to a nearby vendor.

Rianne bit her lip to keep back the tears which had been quite easy to summon when she considered his betrayal. He hated her participation in manly sports. He had to be leading her into a trap. How could he?

Before Lord Robert looked back to check on her, Maid Rianne had disappeared.

## Chapter 33: Rianne Returns

Rianne ran into her rescue party on the way back to camp. Apparently, Lord Petir had riled them up when she had not returned in a timely fashion. William Smythe, Fryer Tuck, Big John, and Dale had agreed to go look for her but had not permitted Lord Petir and his crutch to accompany them. As they walked back to camp, she related her visit to the fair, omitting her interaction with Lord Robert.

Mistress Molly, Little John, and Christopher met them at the camp's edge. Rianne faithfully delivered the message from Christopher's parents, sending the two boys off, whooping triumphantly. They ran past Lord Petir hobbling rapidly in her direction.

"'E has been in a regular snit since he got back," intoned Mistress Molly.

Rianne sighed. It had been a painful walk back while she honestly examined her role in her relationship with Lord Robert. She was still sorting it all out and did not welcome Lord Petir's angry presence. Resolutely, she continued forward, halting when they were toe to toe. The rest of the party tactfully moved on.

*Surprise.*

Lord Petir was not angry. He looked relieved. He regarded her searchingly.

"Something happened, didn't it?" he stated. "And you don't want to talk about it, right?"

*More surprise.*

Rianne nodded mutely, hanging her head.

"Then don't talk about it, Maid Rianne. Think about it. Figure it out. And if you want me to, I'll listen when you're ready."

She raised her eyes to his.

He shoved his hands into his pockets as if he did not know what else to do with them. "Fryer Tuck saved some food for you." He stepped aside. "If you want it."

Bewildered, and more than a little relieved, Rianne wordlessly headed toward the galley. A glance over her shoulder showed him standing in the same spot, watching her.

*He is worried about me.* The realization took her by surprise. A novel sensation warmed her, prompting her to call to him. "I would enjoy some company, Lord Petir." After all, what harm was there in a little company?

She waited as he limped over, the pleased smile on his face matching the one that had suddenly appeared on her own.

***

## Chapter 34: Big John

Petir was sitting under a tree, sullenly trying to spin with Mistress Nellie. He looked up at the shadow falling across the yarn he was attempting to make.

"'E is not faithful to her, you know," said Big John.

Petir grunted. "But she rushed out of here this morning to go see him, didn't she? Said she couldn't wait to show Lord Robert what she could do in a dress."

Petir noticed the yarn was beginning to look pretty messy. He threw up his hands in frustration and moved away from the spinning wheel.

"Sorry about that," he said to Mistress Nellie, who was looking more than a little relieved by his departure.

Big John fell in step beside him. "She would be better off with you."

"Who?"

"Who do you think, m'lord? Maid Rianne."

Petir stopped, surprised by the boy's altruism. Big John was crushing on her big time.

Big John looked up. "I know she would never consider me, but a man cannot help how 'e feels." He fell to studying the doodlings he was drawing in the dirt with his staff.

"I know how you feel," said Petir sympathetically. *I know* exactly *how you feel.*

"The thing is I know I be too young, but I still want her happy."

"So do I, BJ. So do I." *Okay, so I'm pissed she chose the betrothed, but I wish I knew if she's safe or not.*

"If you are so worried about her safety, why do you not follow her?" asked Big John.

*How does he know what I'm worried about?* "Are you sure you're only thirteen?"

"Thirteen and a half, m'lord."

Petir leaned on his crutch and looked at his young collaborator. "And, by any chance, do you know the way to the archery contest?"

"No, he does not." Dale walked up behind his friend. "But I know. I could tell you how to get there, but then I would have to kill you." He snickered and nudged Big John. "I guess you will just have to take us with you, m'lord."

Petir looked at the two grinning boys and felt heartened. "We have a fair to crash."

*** *

## Chapter 35: Avoiding a Trap

A cheerful Mistress Nora walked over to where Rianne lurked in the corner of the tavern. Rianne had delivered Christopher and Little John early this morning. Both boys had disappeared right after breakfast, but not before swearing on both their mothers' souls to remain within the boundaries of the fairgrounds.

As it was too early for customers, Mistress Nora wiped her hands on her apron and settled in next to her. She had stashed Rianne's quiver and bow behind the bar for safekeeping until the tournament. The only thing left to do was to wait. Rianne drummed her fingers on the table.

"Worried about the competition?" Mistress Nora asked, rousing Rianne from her thoughts.

Rianne sat up straight. "Not in the way one would expect. I have been practicing. I am ready to compete." She shifted around to face the tavern keeper. "My betrothed says my competing is a selfish act, that I do it for my own gratification."

"Which I am sure you do, but what is wrong with that? Think of all the good that comes from young maidens seeing a strong feminine competitor with skills usually mastered by men."

Allan Lee strode into the tavern, his arms piled high with wares for the day's meals and his face full of worry. Dropping his load on the bar, he drew a chair up and joined them.

"What is it, Allan?" asked his wife.

"Maid Rianne, have you registered for the archery competition yet?" he asked instead of replying.

"Aye, I did, last week, after the qualifying round."

"Are there any other maidens competing?"

"No. It caused quite a stir when I showed up, so I believe I would have heard if there was another female competitor, although I suppose someone new could register today."

"My dear, I heard a couple of the sheriff's men talking over by the market. They were quite early in their cups and not watching their audience. They plan to take you prisoner and use the leverage to demand the outlaws yield."

"They cannot do that!" cried Mistress Nora.

Rianne was horrified. "We must deliver a message to the camp immediately. King Richard has already sent word that the outlaws will be pardoned on Saturday. If I am caught, I can remain a prisoner until then. Somehow, we must tell them not heed the ransom terms."

"If you get caught? There is no reason for that. We can hide you until the pardon is invoked," said Mistress Nora.

"I mean, if I am taken at the contest," said Rianne quietly.

"You would still compete? Foolish girl! Then, surely, you will be lost."

"Only if I compete as a girl. Garbed as a boy, they will not recognize me. I can register under an alias."

Husband and wife exchanged worried glances.

Rianne patted their hands. "Your concern should not be directed toward me but toward the others. How can we get a message through? Most assuredly, the perimeter of the fair will be watched. I cannot leave."

"We could take the message, Mother," said Christopher.

"That's right. We know the way to the camp," said Little John.

"Boys! How long have you been standing there?" demanded Allan.

"Long enough to know Maid Rianne is in trouble, and we can help," said Christopher staunchly.

"Are you sure you know the way?" asked his father.

"Allan!" said Mistress Nora reprovingly. "You cannot be seriously considering them. They are far too young."

"We are not too young, mum. We have done it dozens of times," boasted Christopher.

"Christopher!" said Mistress Nora as Little John gave her son a sharp elbow to the ribs.

"*Ow*! Oh! I didn't mean *dozens* of times. We just went a few—"

"We only went twice... I mean once..." Little John faded under the angry eyes of the adults.

Rianne fought hard to keep her features schooled but ended up having to turn away to hide her mirth.

"Young man, I will deal with you later," said Mistress Nora. "But for right now, if you are both very sure of the way, you must carry the message, and return straightaway so we can confirm it was received. Can you do that and not get caught?"

The two boys nodded vigorously.

"Are you sure?" Rianne put a cautionary hand on her friend's arm. This seemed too great a risk just so she could compete.

"Aye, I believe they can keep the camp safe." She gathered both boys to her bosom in a motherly embrace and hugged them until they squirmed to get free.

"Mother," said Christopher indignantly, "that is not how you treat a wily outlaw."

She sniffed and released them. "Come. We shall discuss what you should say. Allan, find Maid Rianne some manly garb. I shall return directly."

Allan winked, put up a *CLOSED* sign on the tavern door, and headed for their wagon. Rianne was left alone with her thoughts. Despite her intentions, it appeared she would be competing as a lad after all.

She tensed at the sound of footsteps outside. Their conversation revealed only disappointed customers. She ignored the footsteps that followed. Whoever it was would see the sign and leave.

"I thought you said they would be open." A sulky female voice sounded outside the entrance. "Where else can we get ale this early in the morning?"

"I know the owner. I shall see if he is around."

Rianne's heart lodged in her throat as she recognized the speaker. Lord Robert's voice was unmistakable.

## Chapter 36: Friend or Foe?

*Should I run or hide? Is Lord Robert friend or foe?*
Rianne heard his heavy step on the landing.
*Definitely run.* Explanations could wait until later.

Quickly sliding out of her chair, she gathered her skirts, bent in half, and scurried behind the bar, trying to control her breathing as she listened to see if he had entered the tavern. Deciding she was still alone, she slipped into the kitchen, crouched below window level, and stealthily maneuvered toward the rear entrance.

"Well, well, look who we have here." Lord Robert Gisborne stood between Rianne and freedom, smirking at her over the two tankards he held.

Unable to tell if he was angry, she straightened, trying to judge his intentions. She was about halfway between the tavern door and her betrothed. She still had a chance to escape the way she had come.

"You were going to pay for that, were you not, m'lord?" said Rianne. She certainly hoped she portrayed more nonchalance than she felt. Her heart was racing like a fox fleeing a hound.

"That is the least of your worries, m'lady," he said calmly. "I trust your ankle is healed?"

"Healed well enough, thank you." She could make it out of the inn if she could find a way to distract him. "'Tis quite a bit of ale for this hour, is it not, m'lord?"

"Ah, yes, this." He raised the two cups. "One is for a friend. That friend could have been you if you had remained by my side instead of choosing that ridiculous life."

*He is angry.* "What do you want from me?" she asked.

"That which is my due. Some respect, for one." He took a threatening step in her direction. "For you to *not* embarrass me in public, for another."

She backed up a step. "Embarrass you? I mean no disrespect. Archery is harmless sport. It should not embarrass you for me to compete."

"You do not want to cross me, Maid Rianne. I am not a good enemy to have. Renounce this nonsense, and all will be forgiven. But do it now. I shall not make this offer again."

Rianne stared at him, stunned. "What exactly do you want me to renounce?"

"Forget this foolish obsession with the bow and living outside of convention. Give the location of the outlaw camp, and take your proper place by my side. That tidbit of information will put me in good standing with the sheriff, and you will reap the benefits as well."

"Did you find your friend?" The voice Rianne had heard earlier was attached to the blonde head poking through the kitchen door behind Rianne. It belonged to a voluptuous girl dressed as a scullery maid.

The proper place by Robert's side was starting to look a little crowded.

The blonde stepped into the kitchen and caught sight of the ale. "Ooh, is that for me?"

"I believe it is," said Rianne. She grabbed the girl by the arm and swung her toward Rianne's now-former betrothed. The girl staggered into the red-faced Robert, splashing ale all over them both. He shoved her aside, trying to cut off Rianne's escape, but she bolted back into the bar and out the front door before he had even regained his footing.

## Chapter 37: True Winners

Robert roared behind her, but Rianne did not falter. Racing between horses and people, she tried to put distance between them, hampered by her skirts at every turn. The forest was not an option. She could not risk leading him to her friends. How was she going to disappear in the fairgrounds with guards everywhere?

*The kissing booth! Gypsy Ana will hide me.*

Rianne took refuge in a nearby vendor's booth. She peeked through the clothing on displayed, stepping back to casually examine a rakish black bodice as a guard walked by. Fryer Tuck had been right. No one gave a second glance towards a maid dressed as a maid ought.

*Hmmmm. Now this garment would make my ex-betrothed quite angry.*

She surreptitiously perused the area. There was no sign of Robert. It appeared safe to venture out. With one last check, she headed for the Gypsy's wagon. Hugging the fringe of the fair, darting in and out of booths, she eventually wound her way around to the residential wagon kept behind the kissing booth by her elderly friend. Stealthily, Rianne crept up the wagon stairs and let herself inside. Intent on closing the door silently, she did not realize she was not alone until it was too late.

"How many times do I have to tell you?" said Robert as he hauled her against his muscular body and clamped his hand over her mouth. "I always win."

With her arms pinned by her sides, she futilely struggled, but he was too strong for her.

"Stop it! You are coming with me," he said in her ear. "There will be no cries for help, or your Gypsy friend will become a guest of the sheriff as well. Do you understand me?"

Rianne closed her eyes and acquiesced. She no longer had any illusions about Robert's scruples. She would not compromise Gypsy Ana any further.

Robert reached for a scarf hanging on the wall and bound her hands behind her back.

"Let us take a little walk, you and me." He tightened her restraints and helped her to the ground. "Quietly now. You do not want to raise suspicions." He casually draped his arm over her shoulder, effectively shielding her bonds from view.

"Where are you taking me?"

"Since you will not tell me the location of the outlaw camp, you can tell the sheriff."

"This is not the way to the sheriff. This is the way to the forest."

"Yes, well, I do not want to risk you making a scene in public, so we are going around the fair instead of through it."

"I will not tell him where they are. You should know that about me."

"Most likely," he agreed serenely as they walked out of the fair toward the brush at the end of the clearing. "But by the time he is done questioning you, the archery contest will have concluded."

Rianne stopped and stared at his smirking face. *He would go to such lengths?* Despite the summer heat, she felt chilled to her very bones.

"I warned you not to cross me, Rianne. A true winner does not let anything interfere with his goal. You will come to thank me for this."

"Thank you for this?" *I have had enough.*

Rianne shoved her shoulder into Robert's ribs. He staggered to the side at the unexpected blow. She leaned over, raised a tucked leg, and slammed her heel into his chest. As he tumbled backward, she dropped to the ground to slip her bound hands underneath her and over her feet so they would be in front. Unfortunately, the simple maneuver was hindered by her skirts.

She was up and running, trying to reach the sanctuary of the forest, but the delay caused by untangling her skirts from her bonds had shortened her head start. Robert was right on her heels. Within moments, he seized her around the waist and grappled her to the ground.

Robert stood up, breathing heavily. He was built for smashing, not running. He dusted his hands off with distaste. Rianne lay on the ground, glaring at him. He brushed off his clothing, ignoring her.

"You are trying my patience, Rianne." He reached down, grabbed her by the arms, and pulled her to her feet. "I am taking you to the sheriff, and there is nothing you can do about it."

"You are not taking Maid Rianne anywhere she does not wish to go." Lord Petir leaned on his crutch, fierce determination on his face.

Rianne went cold inside. *Oh, no. Lord Robert is going kill him!*

\*\*\*

## Chapter 38: Securing the Betrothed

"What's this? A crippled criminal? The sheriff is going to love me when I deliver two outlaws to him," taunted Rianne's captor.

"How about three outlaws, Lord Gisborne?" Big John stepped out from behind a tree.

"Or four?" added Dale, standing up from behind a bush.

"Seriously?" Gisborne looked incredulously at the boys, then began to laugh. "Don't tell me you kids have come to rescue the fair maiden. Cute, but not happening." He shoved Maid Rianne to the side, where she stumbled and fell, unable to catch herself with her hands bound.

Even as Petir automatically put out a hand to restrain Big John, a calmness of purpose filled him. A change within had begun when he saw this knight, the size of a linebacker, tackle Rianne. This jackass was going down.

"*You,* I'll deal with later," Gisborne said harshly to Rianne. He shrugged his brawny shoulders and turned toward the others.

"Three against one? I like the odds." He began pushing up his sleeves.

"This is madness," cried Maid Rianne. "He is obviously injured, and surely you would not strike a child!" Rianne's face registered shock and fear as she got to her feet.

Petir felt the same way. How was he supposed to defend her against this pumped-up hulk? With his mind frantically searching for strategies, he managed to quip, "So, this guy's name is Shirley?"

Encouraged by his calm humor, the boys snickered, enraging Rianne's captor. But it was Rianne's responding grin that bolstered Petir's nerve.

"You will regret your insolence, knave," Gisborne growled. "We will see how impudent you are after I take you all to the sheriff. Your days of playing outlaw are over."

"You are not taking her," Petir said firmly. "And you are not taking us."

"And who is going to stop me?" Gisborne sneered. "A bound girl? The boys? You? A cripple?"

"At least we have our honor," said Dale as he sidled into Petir's view.

"Honor? Right. That's a good one. What else would a loser say?"

Gisborne pretended to lunge in Dale's direction, mocking the boy with laughter as Dale scurried out of reach. The ever cocky Gisborne did not notice that Dale's scrambling had placed him closer to Rianne. Nor did he notice he now had his back to Petir.

But Petir noticed. He also observed Big John slowly moving to flank Gisborne on the opposite side. *So that's how it's going to be.*

"You, m'lord, are no better than a diseased cur," retorted Dale, keeping Gisborne distracted.

"Oh, good one, kid." Gisborne's voice dripped with sarcasm.

"He is not a baby goat," corrected Big John from behind him.

As Petir stepped closer, Gisborne suddenly realized Maid Rianne's three young allies had surrounded him. His smug expression turned to a scowl. He changed tactics.

"M'lady, surely you would not strike at me, your betrothed." He turned to her with an insincere smile.

*Thor's evil twin is Rianne's betrothed?* Petir was stunned. *How did she end up with such a jerk?*

Gisborne took a step toward her, but even though her hands remained bound, she nimbly stepped out of grabbing range. Petir and the boys protectively stepped closer, maintaining their positions. Petir remained at Gisborne's back where he could keep an eye on Rianne.

"No, most likely *I* would not," Rianne replied. "However, Lord Robert, I do believe they would." She nodded at her three allies. "And stop calling me Shirley." She grinned at his scowling countenance; the three outlaws chortled in agreement.

After a moment of considering his options, Gisborne composed his face and began pushing down his sleeves. "We seem to be at an impasse. I cannot take you prisoner, nor are you capable of taking me."

He smoothed his jerkin and cracked his neck, slamming his head first to the left, then right, and then rolling his broad shoulders. "It matters not." Suddenly, he was all smug swagger again as he turned toward Maid Rianne. "You have already lost. I merely have to await your departure from the fair and then follow you back to your hideout." He casually flicked something off his sleeve. "Ah, well, I am afraid that is the price you pay for the path you have chosen."

Mocking her, Gisborne tipped his head. "One way or another, m'lady, I shall be seeing you this evening."

She paled at his words. The boys looked anxiously at Petir, acknowledging the truth of his statement.

"Ah well," Petir said, imitating Gisborne. "Then I am afraid you must be detained, m'lord." He resolutely set his shoulders and adjusted his stance for the inevitable.

Gisborne chuckled and began rolling up his sleeves. "I'm going to enjoy teaching you a lesson, you bast—"

Before he could turn around, Petir took his crutch and neatly swung it at the back of the legs of Maid Rianne's betrothed. Gisborne's knees buckled as Petir swept his feet out from under him. He landed on the ground with a decided thud. Big John and Dale each dove onto a muscled arm, momentarily pinning him down.

Petir pointed the tip of his crutch at his throat. "Yield, Lord Gisborne," he said quietly.

"Or what? You're going to stab me with your crutch?" Gisborne jeered.

"You are smart enough to know a staff such as this can crush your throat." He shrugged. "That's why you don't struggle."

Gisborne sullenly relaxed back onto the forest floor, acknowledging defeat.

"Now what?" asked Big John.

"We truss him up like the pig he is," suggested Maid Rianne.

Petir looked at her in surprise. "How did you get untied?"

"I can also be quite clever, m'lord." She removed lengths of braided yarn from her hair, tied them together, looped around Lord Gisborne's thick wrist, and pulled it taut.

"*Oww!*"

"You will find no sympathy here, Knave Robert," she bit out. "I cannot believe you would take me prisoner to prevent me from competing." She ran the line between his legs and around his waist, jerking it to remove the slack.

"Oof!" grunted Lord Gisborne.

*Ouch!* Petir noticed the two boys looked as surprised as he was by her vigor.

Securing his second brawny hand with the end of the yarn, Rianne attached it behind his back, once again pulling it tight. She then took the scarf that had previously bound her wrists, looped it around his neck and tied it to the cord behind him.

"I suggest, Lord Robert, you do not pull on your restraints. You may damage the family jewels," she said sweetly as she got to her feet.

"Wait! You can't just leave me out here in the woods."

"We can, and we will, m'lord." Rianne dusted off her palms. "I am afraid that is the price you pay for the path you have chosen."

"This is crazy," cried Lord Robert.

"Don't worry." Petir slipped the crutch back under his arm. "I've spent the night in this forest before. It's not so bad."

He grabbed Rianne's hand and tugged her toward the fair.

"Kid. Hey, kid! Help me out," Robert caught Dale's eye. "You know I wasn't serious before, right? Help me out, and there'll be a pretty penny in it for you."

Dale glanced sideways at Big John and bleated, "N-a-a-a-a-a-a-h."

Robert angrily opened his mouth to retort, but Big John swiftly stuffed in a piece of cloth.

"That should keep you for a while, you over-muscled cur." With a grim expression, Big John leaned closer and spoke softly. "You are truly a dog. I know about your dalliances. You do not deserve Maid Rianne. I hope you rot out here."

He stood up and rubbed his hands together over Robert's face. "And do not ask me where that cloth in your mouth has been because you do not want to know."

As Lord Robert Gisborne gagged on the strange-smelling fabric, the two boys ran to join Maid Rianne and Petir. The triumphant band of young outlaws headed for the fair, prepared to test their fate.

## Chapter 39: Understanding Competition

*That* was Rianne's betrothed? Petir couldn't quite wrap his head around it. *I'm not surprised he looks like Thor, but I sure didn't think he'd be such a dick.*

"I thought he loved me," said Maid Rianne. "He knew how much I wanted to compete. I cannot believe he would betray me."

Petir felt vaguely stunned himself.

They squatted behind a bush near the back of the fair, waiting for a chance to sneak in. Dale and Big John had already stolen onto the fairgrounds, but not before promising to find a way to watch her compete in the contest.

The adrenaline rush that had turned Petir into a live-action hero ten minutes ago was rapidly ebbing, leaving him feeling somewhat shell-shocked at his audacity. From the sounds of it, Rianne was experiencing a similar reversal.

*This is really bad timing. She needs to be pumped for the contest.* Petir had to find a way to rev her up again.

Taking Rianne by the shoulders, he gently shook her. "He's a jackass, Rianne. You can do so much better. You *deserve* so much better. How can he not appreciate what an incredible warrior you are?"

She blushed at his words. "Lord Robert knows what it takes to be a top competitor. He is correct when he says I have never been successful." She eased away from his hold. "You are kind, Lord Petir, but you do not understand competition."

She was wrong. He understood competition. Although Ping-Pong could not possibly compare to swinging a sword, the principles were the same. He had to choose his words carefully if he was going to make her hear him.

"I understand enough about competition to know the only one you really compete against is yourself. Win or lose, you have to ask yourself, 'Did I do better this time than I have ever done before?' Who cares if you win against a bush-league opponent if you played your worst? Where's the honor in that?"

"There is none, of course."

"Right, but if you achieve your personal best, who cares if you lose? You have no control over who shows up to compete. You only have control over who *you* bring to compete."

Maid Rianne regarded him with her mouth open, looking slightly dazed at his outpouring of words. "My goodness, Lord Petir. You are going to have to teach me about your Ping-Pong. It has served you well."

Once again, he took her by the shoulders. "Go compete, Maid Rianne. Show them what a true warrior can do."

Maid Rianne took a deep breath and nodded. Unexpectedly, she placed her hands on his cheeks, drew his face down to hers, and kissed him soundly. "I will win this tournament for you, m'lord." Grabbing her discarded bow and quiver, she darted into the fair, leaving him reeling.

*What just happened? Rianne just kissed me?* He touched his mouth. *I love this dream!*

Adjusting his crutch, he confirmed there were no prying eyes and began hobbling toward a bush closer to the fair. It felt like he was reenacting a slow version of *Assassin's Creed. Everything's a Lie. Everything's Permitted.* With the X-Box quote running through his mind, he checked the fair's perimeter from the new bush, selected another one for cover, and began watching for a pause in the activity.

*Now!* He was scrambling for the shrub when he spotted a guard. Petir threw himself behind the bush and froze, heart pounding, trying to breathe quietly while listening for any indication he had been detected.

*I'm supposed to be geodashing on my vacation. Instead, I'm bush-dashing in my dream. Go figure.* After what seemed an eternity, he decided to part a couple of branches and peer through.

*Great! I'm hiding behind Lover's Lane.* Frustrated, Petir watched the guard trying to steal a kiss from a teasing young maid. *Couldn't you pick another wagon to make out behind? I'm going to miss Rianne's match!* He had started to search for other means to reach the fair when he heard a familiar voice.

"What are you doing, you lazy lout?"

His heart froze. How could it be? That sounded like.... Petir cautiously peeked through the bush.

"I told you to keep an eye out for them sneaking in, you cretin!" Lord Robert Gisborne, in an angry-Thor stance, was rubbing his wrists and yelling at the unhappy guard who had been happily making out a moment ago.

"You check over there," directed Gisborne. "I'm going to the archery contest."

*How did he get loose?* Petir had to warn the others. Only two more bushes and he would be safe inside the fair, hidden in the crowds.

He stole another glance. The coast was clear. He limped to the first bush, checked his surroundings, and deemed it safe enough to head for the second one. This bush was right next to a parked wagon. He casually stood up, paused a moment for signs of a problem, and then nonchalantly hobbled around the back.

Success!

*Now all I have to do is make sure Rianne and the boys are safe.*

From the back end of the wagon, he peered around the corner. No one was there. He walked along its side, pausing at the corner to sneak a peek at the front.

"*Arrrrgg!*" was the last thing he heard.

A massive Thor's fist coming at his face was the last thing he saw.

## Chapter 40: The End of a Dream

"He's coming to. C'mon, buddy, wake up."

Someone was snapping his fingers loudly in Petir's ear. His pounding head was eclipsed by a foreboding that something was wrong. Very, very wrong. What was it? He moved his head fretfully as he bounced around.

"That's it, buddy. Now open your eyes for me."

He froze inside. The accent was American.

Petir's eyes flew open. He found himself strapped onto a gurney in an ambulance with a flashlight in his eyes as a medic checked his vital signs.

The dream had finally ended. Horror filled him.

He would never see Rianne again.

## Chapter 41: The Intervention

*Bam! Bam! Bam!*

"Dude, open up!"

Petir dragged himself out of bed and over to the door, knowing Beavis and Butt-head would not quit until he let them in. He unlocked his bedroom door, then turned around and belly-flopped onto his bed.

"Dude," began Chris, slumping into the room's only chair. "You need some company." Half a foot shorter than Petir, his frame still overflowed the small seat.

Jimmy thumped Petir on the back before taking his customary seat on the floor. He sighed and propped his back against the bed. As a child, Jimmy had been forbidden to sit on the über-expensive couch his mom had purchased after going back to work; he had only been allowed to sit on the floor and lean against it. Jimmy was a creature of habit.

Petir knew they meant well, but he was not ready to discuss the midsummer week's weirdness. He covered his head with his pillow, hoping they'd take the hint and leave. They didn't.

"It's polite for company to call first."

"Dude! We live in the same apartment." Chris laughed. "But if you want us to call first, replace your cell phone."

"Yeah, Pete." Petir could hear Jimmy rustling a newspaper as he spoke. "Besides, it's time for you to rejoin the world. You can't call in sick forever."

Petir rolled over and stared at the ceiling. "But I *am* sick. I really don't feel well." And he certainly didn't have the energy to get out of bed.

"You're not sick. You're stupid."

"Shut up, Chris," he said automatically.

Chris cleared his throat and deepened his voice. "It is our considered opinion something happened on that vacation, which you took... alone... *without* your best friends to look out for you."

"You were busy."

"Why won't you tell us what's going on?" asked Jimmy, pushing up his glasses.

"Yeah, dude. Get it off your chest, and go back to work."

"Shut up, Chris," said Jimmy.

"What? No work equals no money. No money equals no rent. No rent equals no apartment. You don't want to prove our folks right, do you, Pete?"

"Shut up, Chris," said Jimmy and Petir.

Petir dropped his pillow onto his face. The bed jostled as Jimmy lurched to his feet and sat on the edge. He plucked the pillow off Petir's face.

"Pete, whatever happened, she's not worth it."

*Yes, she was.* Petir took back the pillow, replaced it on his face, and sighed. "I'm fine. And I never said anything about a *she*."

"Dude, of course there's a *she*," snorted Chris. "*Shes* have been knocking mankind on their collective butts since the beginning of time."

"I've known you since third grade. You're better, but you're not fine," said Jimmy.

The bed bounced, indicating Chris was sitting next to Jimmy. "At least you started washing again," said Chris encouragingly. "Dude, you need to snap out of the doldrums. Get moving. Get your blood circulating."

"Yeah, come out with us." Jimmy fetched the discarded newspaper from the floor. "Check this out. It's something called a Renaissance Fair. They dress up like King Arthur and his court and do old-time sports."

Petir sighed for the billionth time, pushed the pillow aside, and reached for the newspaper.

"Aha! A spark of life!" said Chris as Petir read the advertisement.

*King Arthur's court is not Nottingham, but it could be cool, immersed in something like that.* He reached for his pillow.

Jimmy snatched it out of reach. "So you went geodashing and fell out of a tree. So you ended up in the hospital. So your vacation went a little awry. Suck it up, and take it like a man."

"*Awry*? Dude, who talks like that?"

"Shut up, Chris," said Jimmy.

"Hey, check it out!" Chris snatched the paper out of Petir's hand. "They have a kissing booth. Maybe Miss America will be there."

"As long as they've got a Miss Hottie there, I don't care where she's from." said Jimmy. "C'mon, Petir."

*That's 'Maid Hottie.'* Going with them would be a colossal mistake. A Renaissance Fair would only to make him think about Rianne, which, of course, was all he'd been doing since he got home. It was amazing how detailed the memory of his dream was.

Petir cleared his throat. "I don't think so. I have some reading I should do before classes start."

His friends burst out laughing.

"C'mon, Pete. Get over yourself, man! It's been three weeks. We've let you sulk long enough."

"Right! Me and Jimmy are not taking no for an answer." Chris sounded unusually firm. "Consider us your crisis team. This is an intervention."

"Thanks, but no thanks."

Chris and Jimmy exchanged glances.

*Uh-oh.*

His friends jumped off his bed, grabbed the end of his mattress, and heaved. He slid off and hit the floor, tangled in a pile of linens and enjoying his first good laugh since forever.

"Are you coming with us, or are we going to have to hold your defenseless mattress hostage?" demanded Jimmy, peering around the side of the square prisoner.

"All right! All right." He grinned despite himself. "You guys win. I'll do anything to save my defenseless mattress."

"Now that's what I'm talking about!" said Chris. "Jackie Chan would be proud, dude."

## Chapter 42: Earning a Kiss

"Ohhh!" cried the cringing bystanders as the knight whacked an unfortunate, but well-padded, volunteer peasant with his staff. Chris and Jimmy flinched with each blow, even though a ring of rope separated them from the action. Petir watched quietly as the knight struck again.

"Whoa!" cried Chris as the knight felled his opponent for the final time.

"The peasant is deserving of your applause for such a noble attempt," shouted the triumphant knight. "Well done, lad," he said as he extended his hand to his fallen opponent.

"There is nothing noble about a knight fighting an inexperienced peasant," muttered Petir.

"Dickhead," intoned Jimmy as they watched the knight strutting around the ring, challenging the crowd for a new opponent.

"It's not that hard," commented Petir. "They can't help but telegraph their next move with their bodies. All you have to do is figure it out." Weird. Why did he know that? From the dream, or from all the hours at table tennis?

"Oh, like you know," said Jimmy. "This isn't Ping-Pong, pal."

"No, 'e is correct, young sir." The knight had overheard them. "You merely have to read when your opponent is going to strike. Which of you peasants is brave enough to accept my challenge?"

"Not me." Chris laughed. "I'm planning on having kids someday."

"A bargain then. If you can land a single blow, you win a kiss from the bonny maid at the kissing booth. "

Petir was too curious "Sure, I'll give it a try." *Let's see what that dream taught me.*

"He's just kidding. Right, Pete? He wants to have children someday, too." Chris was no longer laughing.

"Don't worry, Chris. He won't hit me too hard. It'd be bad business for the fair."

"That it would, young sir, that it would," agreed the knight. "Squire! Fetch the peasant some padding." The knight held up the rope. "Welcome to the list field."

Jimmy put out a restraining hand, but Petir shook it off.

"I got this, Jimmy." He walked toward the assistant lugging a suit of padding.

"Dude, you have a death wish!" called Chris.

The assistant slipped the padding over his head. It more than adequately protected the torso. Petir accepted a staff from the squire and experimentally twirled it. Its balance was different than he remembered from the dream; but then again, this was not a crutch designed specifically for his needs.

"Ready, peasant?" The fierce gleam in his eyes contradicted the knight's polite words.

Petir nodded tersely. What was he doing? This was not looking like his best idea. You can't apply a lesson from a dream to real life. But it was too late to back out. This guy was going to pummel him. Resolutely, he prepared for his beating.

"Begin!"

The knight circled him, his every move oozing confidence and superiority. Petir watched him strut, hoping to dodge the first strike. The knight lunged and smacked him in the ribs.

"Ohhh!" cried the onlookers.

"Hey, Pete, this is a really bad idea," called Jimmy.

"I'm fine." The blow hadn't really hurt. He adjusted his shoulders under the pad, a slight thrill rippling through him. *Did I just figure out that guy's move before he made it?* He went back to studying the knight. It took the knight landing two more blows for Petir to understand his opponent's timing.

*Weird. Did I get all of this from a dream?*

"Dude, enough already. We all think you're brave. Come out of there!" Chris sounded genuinely anxious.

"No, no. I got this." It was time to apply his dream training.

The knight was too cocky, smirking as he moved in for the kill. Petir slowly turned the staff in his hands. When the knight struck again, he was ready. He parried the next hit and produced a satisfying *clang* as he landed a wallop of his own on the armor.

"No way!" shouted Jimmy.

"You rock, dude," yelled Chris.

Petir grinned as the crowd cheered. His gaze never left the knight, but he could tell his buddies were bouncing off each other on the sidelines.

"Beginner's luck," snarled the knight, changing his stance.

"Careful, Pete," called Jimmy. "I don't think that's all an act. He looks really pissed off."

His adversary charged, but Petir sidestepped him. Without preamble, the knight spun and charged again. Petir deflected his staff and began circling him. Maybe he wasn't going to get a beating after all.

His opponent's frustration was becoming obvious. According to Rianne the Dream Warrior, this was the time a fuming combatant would attack rashly. Petir dodged another blow and suddenly found himself in the position he was waiting for. Using his staff, he swiftly swept his opponent's legs out from under him. The knight landed on his back with a crash and lay there, about as threatening as an overturned turtle.

The crowd cheered as Petir's friends jumped into the arena, hollering and pounding him through the padding.

"Where did you learn to do that?" yelled Jimmy.

"Vacation," muttered Petir. "C'mon, you guys. Help me get him up. That armor looks heavy." With a little effort, the three of them managed to right the sullen knight.

"Sire, you have earned a kiss," said Chris with a formal bow.

Acting alarmed, Petir raised his palms and backed up a step. "I think you're getting a little too excited there, buddy."

"Not from me, dude. You have a date with a bonny maid at the kissing booth."

"Hey, Knight," yelled Jimmy. "He hit you twice. That means two kisses, right?"

The crowd applauded its approval.

"Sure. Whatever," said the knight sourly.

"Let's go collect your reward, dude."

"Oh, man." Jimmy excitedly punched Petir in the arm. "That was so *Kung Fu Panda*."

"No, no," said Chris. "That was so Bruce Lee."

"No way, man," declared Jimmy. "You just made Jackie Chan proud!"

"Ah, the ultimate praise." Chris paused, palms together, to bow serenely at Jimmy. Jimmy pressed his own palms together and solemnly bowed back.

Petir enjoyed their antics, but he was only half paying attention. His mind was wrestling with the million dollar question. How could a dream possibly have prepared him for doing battle? He had eliminated the possibility of it being his Ping-Pong training. Although the sport developed the reflexes, moving a staff required two hands, an entirely different set of skills than swinging a paddle single-handed.

"We're going to call you Lord Petir from now on," chortled Jimmy.

"No!" snapped Petir. That's what Rianne had called him. He did not need another reminder of what he could not have.

A puzzled frown furrowed Jimmy's brow. He slanted an anxious look Chris's way, but Chris shrugged, his own confusion evident.

*Be cool. Be cool, or they'll think you've flipped.* The last thing he needed was to raise more warning flags. His friends would never let him be unless he could convince them everything was fine.

"Uh, *sire* will suffice," he amended with an awkward sweeping bow.

"Yes, sire." Jimmy sounded relieved as he and Chris swept into answering bows.

"Whoot! Whoot! That's what I'm talking about," yelled Chris. "Let's find that kissing booth!"

## Chapter 43: The Woman of His Dreams

"What's wrong?" asked Jimmy uneasily after retracing his steps to the spot where Petir had suddenly rooted.

Petir could not find his voice. He took a deep, shaky breath. *Be cool. Be cool. You can figure this out.*

"Petir?" His friend put a tentative hand on Petir's shoulder. "Are you okay?"

All he was able to do was to draw another shaky breath.

"Hey, Chris!" Jimmy called out. "Something's wrong with Petir."

Chris turned and immediately began to work his way back through the crowd.

"Jimmy," Petir managed to gasp. "I have to talk to that lady." Feeling like his head was going to explode, he pointed a wobbly finger at the hostess of the kissing booth.

"Sure, Pete, sure. Whatever you want." Jimmy nodded to Chris, who ran off toward the booth as if he didn't know what else to do. "C'mon, let's walk over there. It's nice and shady. You'll feel better when you get out of the sun."

Petir ignored him, his eyes transfixed on the hostess.

Still, Jimmy had no trouble steering him over, blathering as they walked. "We shouldn't have pushed you to come out, Pete. The sun is pretty hot. I'll get you a cold drink." Jimmy's voice sounded like controlled panic. "That'll help. Yeah, iced tea. You'll feel fine after you sit for a while."

"Excuse me, ma'am," Chris was saying. "My friend hasn't been feeling well lately, and he needs to speak with you."

The elderly hostess in the colorful skirt raised her head and smiled as her impish eyes met Petir's. "I imagine he does," she said in her musically foreign voice.

Gypsy Ana winked at Petir.

Petir quietly freaked out.

## Chapter 44: LARPing

"Dude, what is going on?" asked Chris nervously.

The mysterious woman had just disappeared into the colorful wagon. Jimmy put out a hand to stop Petir from following.

"He's right, Petir," he said firmly. " Seriously. You are not going anywhere until you tell us what the hell is going on."

Seeing Gypsy Ana again was totally freaking Petir out. *I might as well tell them the whole thing. They think I'm nuts right now anyway.*

"Look, you know I had a little…accident while I was on vacation."

Chris was frowning, his arms folded across his chest. Suddenly reminded of the guy's dad, Petir had to suppress a mildly hysterical urge to giggle like a girl.

"I'm fairly certain I was unconscious for a time, and while I was out," he paused to consider his words. "I had this weird dream. It was so incredibly realistic that I…that's not important. What *is* important is that woman was in my dream."

"Who? The Gypsy lady?" asked Jimmy. "No way."

"Dude, maybe you met her some place before and don't remember," suggested Chris.

"Seriously? Do you forget the Gypsies you meet?"

"Fine. If you want to believe you dreamed about a real live person you never met before, go ahead," retorted Chris. "It could happen. You see things like that in horror movies."

"Shut up, Chris," said Jimmy. "Are you sure it was her, Pete?"

"Oh, I'm positive. I'm seriously freaking out right now."

"What is she? A witch?" asked Chris. "Maybe she put a spell on you or something."

"Shut up, Chris," said Petir automatically as he pushed past his companions and headed toward the wagon. "I have no idea what she is, but I'm going to find out." He stopped at the top of the wagon stairs and turned to his friends, who were crowding behind him. "Guys, I got this, okay?"

"No way, dude. We're coming with you. Right, Jimmy?"

Petir blinked in surprise. He had never seen Chris so resolute. Jimmy stood firm behind him.

"Fine. You can come in, but you can't talk."

"Yeah, okay," said Jimmy. "We can do that, right?" Jimmy punched Chris in the back. Chris became an instant bobble-head of agreement.

Petir braced himself and stepped through the doorway. "I'm going to have a nervous breakdown."

The aging Gypsy sat behind a small table which was covered with white lace and topped with a glass ball. She had draped a lacy black shawl over her head—the quintessential Gypsy shrouded in mystery. She gestured for him to sit across from her and waved the others toward chairs on the side.

"Hi," said Chris. "I'm Chris, and this is Jimmy, and that is—"

"Petir Rojo Capota. Yes, I know." She gazed calmly at Chris, who blinked back at her in surprise.

*Hah!* The oddest feeling surged through Petir. *I didn't make her up. She knows my name.* But should that tidbit of info be making him feel better or worse?

"And you are…?" Chris hinted.

"Ahh, here I am known as Miss Ana, but I have gone by many names. Sit, please."

Having no idea where to begin, Petir lowered himself into the chair opposite the elderly woman. He stared at her in silence, his stomach roiling.

"So, Petir," she prompted. "Would you like to explain what happened?"

"Are you kidding me right now?" Petir shot to his feet, toppling his small chair. "You want *me* to explain? To you? Seriously?" Petir pushed his palms into his forehead. "What the hell is going on?"

Jimmy reached out and put a hand on Petir's shoulder—whether restraining or supporting, Petir couldn't tell. He shrugged it off and leaned on the table, looming over the small woman.

"I *dreamed* you. You were in this dream I had after an accident." It did not help Petir at all to see Gypsy Ana's face register surprise. If a Gypsy didn't get it, it was going to go beyond weird.

"Dude," breathed Chris.

"Shut up, Chris," snapped Petir.

"No, he's right, Pete," said Jimmy.

He spun toward them. "Look, if you two can't be quiet, I'm kicking you out."

They held up their palms in a surrendering gesture and leaned back in their seats. Petir turned to the Gypsy.

"I dreamed you up. And I dreamed up a band of outlaws…and the most amazing girl in the world." Petir stood up. "I sound crazy." He covered his eyes with his fingers. "Maybe I'm going crazy.'

"You not crazy. It was not a dream. You were there, truly, as was I, and Maid Rianne."

Petir stared at her for a moment, his mouth hanging open. *It was real? Maid Rianne is real?*

"Who's Maid Rianne?" asked Chris, sitting up straighter.

"Shut up, Chris. You're going to get us kicked out of here," hissed Jimmy.

The Gypsy patted the table. "Sit, dear boy. Please, describe your accident. Perhaps I can help with the rest, yes?"

The events of the past week began to haphazardly tumble around in his head. If it was possible, he felt crazier than before. Heart pounding, he righted the chair and sat down.

"I don't know exactly what happened. I was geodashing with my cell phone, and I lost my signal. So, basically, *I* was lost. I climbed a tree to find the road. The branch I was on broke off, and I fell."

"Dude," murmured Chris.

"Shhh," said Jimmy.

"So, it was getting dark, and my hamstring was too hurt for me to walk out of there. I had to wait 'til morning. I guess I fell asleep because when I woke up, I was surrounded by a pack of mini Robin Hoods. Everyone had a British accent. It was too bizarre to be real, so I figured I was just dreaming."

"No way!" said Chris.

Petir turned toward his friends. "I was confused, okay? I don't know why it made sense at the time, but it did. I kept thinking I was going to wake up, but every morning, I was still there."

"Still where?" asked Chris. "Exactly where were you?"

"I don't know. At the end, I think I got knocked out in a fight, and I woke up in an ambulance, back in my own time."

"Why didn't you tell us?" Jimmy reproached.

"Tell you what, exactly? That I had a *really* long dream? Or that somehow I had lost a week? Or that I don't know where I was for most of my vacation? Which one sounds best to you?"

"Good point."

"Then I come to this fair and see Gypsy Ana here in my world. Now I'm more messed up than before."

"Me, too," chimed in Chris.

"Miss Ana, do you have any idea what happened to me?" he begged.

She nodded and leaned back. Filled with relief, he sank into his chair, watching her tap her fingertips together as she muttered, "Where to start? Where to start?"

She leaned forward. "Petir, do you know the LARPing? No? Live Action Role Playing, yes? LARPers are people who play a role from a story and live the life their character would live.

"During the fair in Guilford, there is a contest, independent. With two LARPing teams, yes? LARPers put money into a pot to be divided amongst the winners. The sheriff's team must locate the outlaw camp to win, but the outlaws win by remaining hidden." She paused for a moment, allowing her words to sink in.

"Cool," murmured Chris.

Jimmy poked him in the ribs.

"You were found by the children of the outlaw camp, no? They forage in the woods, yes? You meet my good friend, Dr. Aileen Jenkins. She determined you did not need a hospital, and you yourself said no one was expecting you. The elders, they decide to let you stay, yes? You had the heart of a LARPer. No one suspect, dear boy, you did not understand where you were, or what they were doing."

Petir had to ask. "So Maid Rianne is real?"

"Who's Maid Rianne?" asked Chris

"Shut up, Chris," chorused Jimmy and Petir.

The elderly Gypsy patted Petir's hand. "Yes, she is as real as you or I. As a matter of fact, she lives here in Connecticut."

Elated, Petir stopped breathing. *Oh, yes! This is perfect! Rianne lives in Connecticut!*

He dropped his head into his hands. *Oh, no. This is awful. Rianne lives in Connecticut. What was I thinking?* He wasn't Lord Petir in this realm. He was Petir, the computer geek. This was way worse than thinking she was a dream. She was real, and he didn't dare seek her out.

"Where does she live?" asked Chris.

"Shut up, Chris," snapped Petir.

"'Twould not be appropriate for me to reveal where she lives. However...." She lifted the lace off of the glass ball and, leaning forward, began to weave her hands in the air. "What kind of Gypsy would I be if I could not tell you where she is at this very moment?"

With a mixture of dread and anticipation, he watched the elderly woman close her eyes and gently rock to and fro, her hands poised over the crystal ball. Suddenly, she opened her eyes and leaned forward. So did her three guests.

"She is here."

## Chapter 45: Nothing to Lose

Petir scrambled to his feet. "What do you mean, she's here?" Dread was rapidly morphing into panic.

"At this very festival." Miss Ana peered more intently into the crystal ball. "Ah, yes. The fair maiden is preparing to compete in the archery contest, even as we speak, on the far side of the fairgrounds."

"Your crystal ball told you all that?" Chris's voice was filled with awe.

The Gypsy oozed mischief. "Truthfully, no. We shared breakfast this day." She chuckled.

"Let's go find us an archery contest," said Chris excitedly, getting ready to jump out of the wagon.

Petir grabbed his arm. "I can't go over there!"

"Sure you can."

"What if she sees me?"

"Duh. That's the point, idiot. What's with you?" said Jimmy.

"I can't just go over there," insisted Petir. "She knows this guy I was in the dream. She doesn't know *me*. I acted that way because Miss Ana said I only had a fortnight to rescue her. Don't you get it? I didn't think any of it was real. I thought it was all a dream. *That wasn't the real me.* I only acted that way because I thought it wasn't real."

"That was not the *real* you?" Miss Ana looked puzzled. "So it was the fake you who sat with her by the fireside? It was the fake you who went to her rescue?"

"You rescued her? Dude, that's so cool. Rescued her from what?" said Chris.

"Shut up, Chris," said Petir. "I didn't rescue her. I got beat up, okay?"

"No, Pete, he's right. That's totally cool," said Jimmy.

"Shut up, Jimmy," said Petir.

"The choice is yours, m'lord." Miss Ana slapped her thighs and stood slowly, slyly looking at him as she made ready to leave the wagon. "You have only thirty minutes, my dear boy. Is not a lot of time, in this world or the dream world. When the contest ends, she will go her way, and you will never see her again." She paused in the doorway and spoke more gently "Remember this. *She* only acted the way she did because she thought it *was* real." With that, she stepped out of the wagon.

Chris jumped out of the wagon behind her. "C'mon, Pete! Let's go, dude."

"I'm not going."

Jimmy began herding him down the wagon stairs. Petir dug in his heels when he reached the ground. "I don't want to see her."

"Who cares if you want to see her?" said Jimmy. "*I* want to see what she looks like."

"No way, guys. I'm staying here."

"Petir, seriously, dude, you have been beyond drooling for this girl since you got back."

"Yeah, we thought you were sick."

"C'mon, dude! You got nothing to lose," said Chris.

"It wouldn't work out. You don't know her. She's like Xena. She kept attacking me with her staff. And she has a boyfriend who looks like Thor. And she is totally opposite everything geeky." *I'm babbling.*

"Jeez, Pete. She really got to you," said Jimmy. He draped a sympathetic arm over his shoulder. "I understand completely if you don't want to go over there. These things take time. We both understand. Right, Chris?"

"Yeah, we understand, dude," said Chris. "Completely. We're here for you, Pete." He delivered a slap on the back which made Petir stagger. "We'll just meet you back here after."

"Yeah, no problem," said Jimmy. "We can figure out which one she is without you."

"Later!" cried Chris.

Petir staggered under a second slap on the back from Jimmy before his two former best friends bolted. He stood there with his mouth hanging open. *What just happened?*

Miss Ana walked over and nudged his jaw closed. "No matter, young man. You not ready to risk in this realm. I am sure you will find someone else just like her when you are."

"Just like Rianne? Are you kidding? There is no one like Rianne. That kind of girl wouldn't want to be with someone like me."

"Someone like you? You refer to someone who listen when she talk? Someone who encourage her dreams? Someone who keep her safe from danger?"

"The danger wasn't real."

"Ah, but you did not know."

"Look, I'm no warrior. Her boyfriend knocked me out with one punch."

"Next time, duck."

"Ha ha."

"You felt worthy enough to pursue when you thought it was all a dream. What is the difference?"

He sighed. "You just don't get it. When I didn't think any of it was real, I had nothing to lose."

"And what do you have to lose now?"

Petir opened his mouth to reply, then closed it. What did he have to lose? There was no risk of losing Rianne. He didn't have her in the first place. It certainly wasn't a matter of protecting his feelings. He'd been feeling like crap ever since he returned home.

"I have nothing to lose," he murmured. Hope rushed in, crowding the panic previously ruling his chest. Why not? Abruptly, he swept the small Gypsy into a bear hug.

"I have nothing to lose!" This time he shouted it to the world as he twirled her in a circle.

She laughed as he gently set her down. She reached up and pressed her thumb on his forehead. "You will find much happiness, Petir Rojo Capota. Now go to her."

"Um, right. Right! Which way?"

He dashed off toward the indicated direction, brimming with excitement and possibility, with only one thought in mind.

*Find Rianne.*

## Chapter 46: The Archery Contest

So, this was how Rianne spent her time.

A crowd had already gathered along the ropes close to the contestants. Petir had arrived too late to get very close. The only open spot he could find along the ropes was closer to the targets where the crowd thinned out, but it was good enough. From there, he could see the four contestants on his right, and, to his left, he could view the four padded white targets covered with red concentric rings.

The contestants were busily setting up their equipment or stretching. All of them, that is, except for the only female competitor, Rianne. Unlike the other hopefuls, Rianne had her back to the archery arena.

*Uh oh. Something's not right.* The realization unceremoniously shoved all of Petir's worries about seeing Rianne into the background.

Judging from the set of her shoulders, she was very upset. Craning his neck gave him only a slightly better view, but it was enough. He could see someone had her by the arm, but Lady Big-Hat blocked the rest of the picture.

The announcer began to introduce the archers.

*What the hell? They're starting, and Rianne's not even paying attention.* As he watched, she eventually shook off the hand on her arm and turned around in time for her own introduction. She grimly curtsied to the applauding crowd and turned back to whoever was upsetting her. A hand shot out, grabbed her arm, and abruptly pulled her out of his sight.

Before he could head up there to see if she needed help, she reappeared, tense and pale. Petir had been too preoccupied with

Rianne to see her competition's first shots. He watched her while she watched the third archer shoot. Then it was her turn.

The audience cheered as the only maiden stepped forward to compete. His heart banged against the walls of his chest. She was magnificent, dressed in a flowing period dress of dark blue, her hair cascading down her back. But everything was wrong. This was not Warrior Princess Rianne. This Rianne was biting her lip in uncertainty. Even at this distance, he could tell she was unfocused and distracted. *What the hell is going on? Who's messing with her up there?*

She notched her arrow, aimed, and shot. The crowd let out a sympathetic groan as her missile sailed by the target. She stared at the target for a moment, then stepped back to wait her next turn. A slight ripple of applause reached out to support her, but judging from her drooping shoulders, it was ineffective. Her hair created a curtain around her face, preventing him from seeing her expression.

His heart ached for her as he hurriedly checked out how her competition had fared. All three had hit the target within the outer two rings. The first contestant was up again.

Petir looked back at Rianne. She was watching in a disinterested, detached way, as if all energy had drained out of her. Both the first and the second contestants showed a slight improvement with their second shots. Petir checked out Rianne as the third contestant stepped forward. She was listlessly reaching for her bow. As soon as the shot was fired, she stepped forward for her second turn. Everything about her telegraphed, "Let's get this over with."

"Petir! Hey, *Petir*!" Chris shouted over the crowd. "She's really hot! No wonder you've been moping around."

Behind Jimmy's hand clamping over Chris's mouth, behind the irritated bystanders turning around to shush Chris, behind it all, Petir saw Rianne's head shoot up, her eyes scanning the crowd. Her face registered shock when she found him. Then, right before his eyes, she transformed into the confident, beautiful warrior he remembered. Eyes flashing, shoulders back, and head held high, she broke eye contact with him and whipped an arrow out of its quiver. With a move as graceful as a ballerina's, she embedded it in the center of the target.

The crowd broke into a rousing cheer. A blushing Rianne stepped back, once again smiling at Petir across the crowd.

"Whoot! Whoot!" Chris and Jimmy had found their way over to Petir. They were alternating between jumping up and down, and pounding him on the back.

"That was *so* hot!"

"I'm going to get me some archery lessons."

"Not from her, you're not." Petir's eyes never left Rianne.

The crowd quieted for the final round of shooting. The throng cheered again as the first competitor struck the ring surrounding the center. The second competitor did not come as close but still hit his best shot. The third shooter was now getting ready. Petir knew all this because of his friends' chatter, but his focus was on the hand which, once again, had grabbed Rianne's arm.

"What's up?" asked Jimmy, catching sight of Petir's scowling face. He followed the look to Rianne. "Hey, Petir, I think that's Thor grabbing her," he said quietly.

"What?"

"You know, her ex-boyfriend who looks like Thor. He's messing with her mind."

"Yeah, dude. I heard him tell her she looked like a dyke with her bow and arrow." Chris looked disgusted. "He's cold, man. He said that's why her new boyfriend dumped her."

"Her *new* boyfriend?" *Rianne had a new boyfriend already?* His heart sunk. *Well, what did you expect?* Of course someone like Rianne would be swept up the second she became available. So much for Miss Ana's "you will find much happiness" prediction. How long had he been burrowing in his room? He definitely needed to sit down with a calendar and figure out what day it was.

"Thor's trying to get her back with the old, 'no one else wants you' ploy," said Jimmy.

"*Ploy*? Dude, who talks like that?" said Chris.

As Petir watched, Rianne angrily shook off the hand holding her arm. It certainly looked big enough to belong to Thor. Despite his own disappointment, he felt proud of her. She was not allowing that jackass to diminish her, not one bit.

It was time for Rianne's last shot. Turning her back on Thor and the crowd, Rianne stepped forward to address the target. She turned her head to find Petir, smiled at him, and without skipping a beat, plunged a second arrow next to her first in the center of the target.

Petir leapt into the air. "*Yeah*! Now that's what I'm talking about!" He pounded Chris on the shoulder. "Did you see that? Did you see that?"

"Oh, yeah, dude. That was totally hot!"

The crowd stomped and cheered as Rianne shook hands with her opponents and the judges. He felt like he was going to bust with pride.

"What do you say, Pete? Want to say hi to an old friend?" Jimmy asked.

"Sure." He squared his shoulders. He was no longer a mere computer jockey. He was a warrior going into battle. And even if it scarred him for life, he knew it wouldn't kill him. He was going to go congratulate Rianne.

They wormed their way through the crowd until they were standing near her. Petir grinned broadly as she accepted her trophy. Watching her gracefully acknowledge the skills of the other archers, suddenly, it didn't matter as much who she chose to be with. Once before, he had decided his mission in life should be to make Rianne laugh. He was now going to modify his mission to making Rianne happy. If being with someone else made her happy, then so be it. If stepping out of her way was what she wanted, he was prepared to do so. If—

Turning her head, Rianne met his eyes with a glowing smile, and Petir promptly lost his train of thought.

## Chapter 47: The Small Rescuer

Rianne took a step through the well-wishers toward Petir, reaching out her hand. Once again, he had no idea what to do. Knowing this moment might never come again, he raised her hand and reverently pressed it to his lips.

Completely poised, she dropped into a graceful curtsey. "M'lord," she acknowledged with an elegant nod and a brilliant smile. "You came."

He smiled back, slightly startled by her American accent. "Maid Rianne, you rock."

*"Rock this, you as—"*

Robert Gisborne's jealous charge came from behind, but it was abruptly halted. Before Petir could even turn, his attacker was on the ground in the fetal position, gasping for air, as the crowd scattered to a prudent distance. Robert didn't look so much like Thor, lying there holding his belly, his mouth open like a goldfish, but that's what a staff to the gut will do to you. Petir knew that feeling all too well.

"Whoa!" yelled Jimmy and Chris as they hopped up and down in excitement. "What just happened?"

Robert's small assailant was twirling her staff as she watched the disbanding crowd move to a safer spot. She reached out a small, dainty foot and soundly kicked Robert in the ribs. Cordelia then rearranged her skirts, calmly leaned on her staff, and waited. Rianne looked on unsympathetically.

"I told you I'd find the black-hearted knave who kicked my dog," said Cordelia.

*"Robert* kicked Trio?" Rianne asked.

"Yeah." Cordelia looked at the crumpled Robert with disdain. "Now you know what it's like to be kicked when you are down, you big bully. Who kicks a three-legged dog anyway?"

Cordelia turned to Petir and prettily extended her hand. "M'lord." She wrinkled her nose impertinently as she curtsied.

His mouth was hanging open. Except for the staff to Robert's stomach, Petir would never have guessed this to be the same Cordelia who had flattened him in the woods. She was completely transformed in her maidenly, forest green dress with her red hair draping in soft waves around her shoulders. Her dress and behavior were old world, but she, too, spoke like an all-American girl

"Wow, Cordelia. You are quite the beauty! Who knew?"

"I knew," said her mother walking up behind them. "But I could never get her to put it on. Not until she saw you go gaga over Rianne's dress. She changed her mind but quick, let me tell you."

"Mom!" Cordelia blushed furiously, but Victoria merely burst out laughing.

"Hey, not bad! With one sentence, not only did I manage to embarrass my daughter, but I made both Rianne *and* Petir blush."

"Lords don't blush," Petir defended good-naturedly as he adjusted to the American sounds coming out of Victoria and her daughter. "And I didn't go gaga over her dress. I was just admiring the way she looked in it."

"I'll just bet you were, *m'lord*," intoned Chris.

"Shut up, Chris," he said good-naturedly.

"I knew she was a beauty." Dale walked up wearing a T-shirt labeled *Coventry Tennis*. He draped an arm over Cordelia's shoulders and leaned on her. "I always knew."

"Ahh, puppy love," sighed Victoria.

"Leave them alone," admonished Rianne, laughing at the two new blushes Victoria's words produced.

Robert groaned from behind them, drawing Victoria's attention. She regarded him lying on the ground, still holding his stomach. Grimly, she folded her arms across her chest. "I do believe someone should tell me what's going on here."

The others exchanged glances as Robert slowly sat up.

"Basically," offered Jimmy, "Thor here got beat up by a girl who was mad he kicked her three-legged dog."

"She should not...be allowed...to carry that weapon," growled Robert between gasps.

Victoria frowned at her daughter. "Cordelia, did you strike this young man?"

"'Tis true, Mum," affirmed Cordelia, slipping back into character. She tried unsuccessfully to project remorse.

"Because he's the one who kicked our injured dog?"

"Yes, Mum."

Victoria mulled that over for a moment. "Let me make sure I understand this. You're in the seventh grade, and you beat up this young man, who is twice your size, because he kicked your three-legged dog, which doesn't even come up to his knee."

"That I did, Mum."

"I see." Victoria squatted in front of Robert. "You could press charges against this little girl who beat you up, but I am fairly certain you could be satisfied with me doling out appropriate punishment for my daughter. What do you think?"

Robert was red-faced. "Sure, sure, why don't you handle it?" he replied, trying to regain his composure as he struggled to his feet.

"Good call, Robert," said Rianne as she shouldered her bow. "Don't piss off any more middle-schoolers. I'm outta here."

"Hold it, Rianne. I'm not done with you yet," Robert snarled.

"But I'm done with you, Robert." She turned to go. "We're history. C'mon, everyone."

"We're history when I say we're history!" Robert made a grab for her arm.

"Hey, back off!" Petir body-checked him, diverting his hand. As Robert stumbled to the side, Petir registered an ache in his shoulder. *Ow! This guy feels like a lumpy boulder.*

Robert regained his balance to find Petir positioned between him and Rianne.

"I'm going to snap you like a twig." His face was red with fury.

"Probably." Dread curled inside Petir. *This is going to be bad.*

Chris and Jimmy came to stand by his side.

"Pete, we got your back, but honestly, dude, I think he can take us," hissed Chris.

Robert took a step toward them. "I'm really going to enjoy this."

"I promise you won't." Cordelia stepped forward, casually balancing her staff as she spoke.

"Oh no, you don't, young lady." Victoria grabbed her arm and hustled her away. "Dale, you're coming, too." Victoria snagged him with her free hand. "Let's make ourselves useful and go find a cop."

Suddenly, Miss Ana stepped in front of Robert. "You do not need officer. I am here." She was slowly weaving strange signs in the air with her hands. "Young man, your future does not include the young lady. I have seen it. You will return home now." Her voice was firm but gentle. She reached up and pressed her thumb on his forehead. "Now go, before I remove my Gypsy blessing and have you escorted out."

Robert stood there for a moment, looking unnerved by the small Gypsy woman staring up at him intently. "Crazy old lady," he muttered. Abruptly, he spun on his heel and left, still muttering.

Miss Ana chuckled and turned to Petir and his roommates. She reached up to pat him on the cheek. "Brave boy. He would have taken you apart, yes? And your two brave friends, yes?"

"Lady," said Chris. "I think you just saved our lives."

"Maybe not." Petir wove his hands in the air as if engaged in some martial art, feeling buoyant after his close brush with a sound beating. "Ooohwwwaaaaahhhhh."

"Ah, yes. Jackie Chan would be proud." Miss Ana chuckled again.

"Wait, what? What did you say?" Petir straightened in surprise.

"Hey, Miss Ana, what's that thing you do with your thumb?" Chris asked.

"Only the Gypsy knows the ways of the Gypsies," she replied in a mysterious tone.

"So, what is it? Some kind of Gypsy blessing?"

"Nah. I like messing with you." She laughed and turned to go. "You come, boys. There are two kisses to be redeemed at my kissing booth."

"Yeah, Pete, let's go," said Jimmy.

"You guys start without me. I'll meet you there."

"What about Maid Rianne?" said Chris with a look that spelled t-r-o-u-b-l-e. "She looks like she could use—"

"Some fried dough," Petir hastily interrupted.

"Whatever, dude." Chris wiggled his eyebrows as Jimmy grabbed him by the arm. They trotted after Miss Ana, leaving Petir alone with Rianne.

He took a deep breath and turned to find her gazing happily at him. Suddenly feeling warmer than the midday sun warranted, he cleared his throat.

"I have a really weird story to tell you."

## Chapter 48: The Folks

"How's my baby?" boomed the knight who, out of nowhere, had scooped up Rianne and was merrily swinging her in a circle.

*Must be the new boyfriend.* Petir's mood soured instantly.

"I am *so* proud of you, sweetheart. I knew you could break that glass ceiling. Two! Dead center!" The knight chuckled heartily.

Petir couldn't see his face, but from behind, the new boyfriend looked like another Thor. *C'mon, Rianne!*

"I have someone I want you to meet," Rianne said breathlessly as Thor Number Two put her down. She grabbed his hand and tugged him around to face Petir, who was busily summoning a polite smile.

"Petir, these are my guardians, Arthur and Gwen King."

Petir's polite smile erupted into a full-blown grin. A graceful woman, clad as a lady-in-waiting, reached around from behind her husband to take Petir's hand.

"M'lady," Petir said formally. "I'm Petir Rojo Capota."

Smiling, she dropped into a graceful curtsy. "So very nice to meet you."

As she stood, her husband extended his hand. "Arthur King, son. Pleased to meet you," he boomed as he pumped Petir's hand. He paused, mid-pump, with his brow drawn. "Just a minute. Are you the same Petir who took down that guy, Gisborne, with only a crutch?"

*Awkward.* "Yeah, well. About that...I can explain."

"Yes, he's the one," said Rianne with a twinkle.

Arthur resumed pumping Petir's hand up and down. "Well done. Well done. No explanations needed. Never did like him."

"King!" admonished Gwen.

"What? He was a bully. I said he was a bully from the start, did I not?"

"Yes, Arthur," chorused Rianne and Gwen.

"But I had to find out for myself," said Rianne. She reached up on tiptoe and kissed Arthur on the cheek.

As she did the same to Gwen, Arthur cleared his throat. "Explanations can wait until tonight. You will join us for dinner, Petir?"

"Tomorrow night," corrected Gwen and Rianne in a cheerful chorus.

"That's right. That's right. Tomorrow night," Arthur repeated

"That is, if you are free, m'lord," said Rianne, her smile marred as she bit her lip.

*So what if she has a new boyfriend. I'm here right now, not him.* "Tomorrow night would be great," answered Petir firmly.

"Lovely," said Gwen. She linked her arm through her husband's and began steering him away. She snared Rianne with her other arm for a loving squeeze and a quick "I knew you could do it!" before they left.

"Be home before eleven," Arthur called over his shoulder. "And have fun with your new boyfriend."

"King!" scolded Gwen as she dragged him away.

Too late. Petir felt deflated. *Rianne sure moves fast.*

He turned to see her reddened face. *At least she's embarrassed about it.*

"I can't believe he said that," Rianne muttered.

"No problem. I understand. Parents, right? I mean, guardians," he ended lamely.

"They're my folks," Rianne said simply. "It's just vocabulary." She grabbed him by the hand. "C'mon, we should talk. You said you have a really weird tale to tell." She smiled as she tugged. "*And* you owe me fried dough."

Petir's heart picked it up a notch.

## Chapter 49: The Real Rianne

Rianne Fitzwater was a regular girl. She had grown up in Connecticut like Petir had, watched the same TV shows, even used the same toothpaste. She would soon be starting her senior year at Coventry High School, which was only fifteen minutes from the University of Connecticut. She was a normal seventeen-year-old American girl, if you considered knowing your way around a bow and staff 'normal'. She was vibrant and alive, and, most importantly, she was real.

He couldn't get used to it. Or her American accent. He watched her snagging another piece of the fried dough he was holding. They were sitting on the back of the kissing booth stage, facing a field, lazily swinging their legs back and forth. A thick red velvet curtain separated them from the antics on the other side. They could hear muffled voices and laughter, but on this side, with the summer breeze cutting across their shaded perch and no one in sight, they felt completely and deliciously isolated from the world.

She leaned forward in an unsuccessful attempt to keep the powdered sugar from falling on its way to her mouth. As she brushed it off of her dress, a pendant swung out of her bodice.

"What's this?" He palmed it, avoiding all parts of her anatomy. He turned the small wooden carving in his hand.

"Hmmm?" She daintily licked her fingertips and looked down. "Oh, that's a 'temporary' gift from Miss Ana." Rianne suddenly blushed. "It's some kind of good luck charm for finding true love. And I quote...." Her voice took on Miss Ana's musical accent. "If it be the anniversary of your birth when you first kiss, that blessed moment over the ancient rune becomes your union of destiny." She wiggled her fingers spookily in the air and laughed.

"What does *that* mean?"

"Basically, if you get kissed on your birthday over the rune, it's true love's destiny. Supposedly some ancient rune was carved into a tree, and a spell was cast on it, I guess. They turned the tree into boards, and used the boards to make this kissing booth. Someone carved this out of one of the boards. Pretty, huh?"

*True love's destiny?* "Do you believe it?"

"Nope. I told her I already had a boyfriend, and my birthday was in January, but she made me take it anyway." She sobered as she studied the carving. "I guess she was right about the boyfriend, though, and she hadn't even met him."

She carefully tucked it away. "I have to remember to return it to her. I don't need it now. Out with the old; in with the new. Right?"

*Ugh. The new boyfriend.* Petir was careful to keep a neutral expression because Rianne was studying him while biting her lip.

"Why did you leave without saying good-bye?" she finally asked.

Petir cleared his throat. "Okay. It's time to tell you my really weird story." He was going for broke, no matter how absurd it sounded.

But first, he just had to get that powdered sugar off her nose. She had a great nose. He reached over and gently swiped the offending sugar away. Her skin felt warm and smooth under his fingers. Funny how something so innocent could make him feel breathless.

She stayed perfectly still until he finished, then cleared her throat. "You, uh, have some on you, too." She leaned over to brush the corner of his mouth with her fingertips.

He registered a faint scent of coconut and summer in her hair before she raised her eyes to his. After that, nothing registered except the fact he was slowly leaning toward her. He froze.

*What are you doing? Be cool. Be cool. New boyfriend. New boyfriend. New boyfriend.*

*Aww, to hell with it.*

Petir kissed her. Her lips were soft and pliant under his, and, wonder of wonders, she was kissing him back.

This was better than a dream.

## Chapter 50: Epilogue

"Happy Birthday, dear Petir. Happy Birthday to you." Petir's grandfather was holding the kitchen door open for his cake-bearing wife, her face lit by the glow of birthday candles. Petir was sure they weren't singing in Spanish because Rianne was there.

"*Abuela, Abuelo,* what are you doing? It's not my birthday. That was months ago. We are going to Rianne's homecoming dance."

"We miss you birthday. You were on the adventure." said his grandfather. "Today, you bring special girl for picture, so today we celebrate."

"Make a wish and blow out your candles, birthday boy," laughed Rianne, adjusting the corsage on her dainty black dress. "When was it really?"

"Almost two months ago," Petir hedged. He took a deep breath and extinguished all the candles at once. He turned and made a sweeping bow in response to the applause from three of the special people in his life. He gazed at Rianne in her homecoming splendor, and his heart did a little quivery thing as he considered what to tell her.

"Actually, it was the day we met," he said to Rianne, wondering how she'd respond.

"You kissed me on your birthday? Why didn't you say anything when I told you about the rune?"

"Because I thought you had a new boyfriend, and I didn't want to mess with you. Besides, I don't believe in that stuff."

Rianne put an arm around Petir's waist. "No, there was no new boyfriend. Uncle Arthur was just teasing me about you. You know Uncle Arthur. He couldn't resist. That was the first time I'd seen you since you left the fair. Without saying good-bye, I might add."

Petir opened his mouth to protest, but she gently covered it with her fingers. "I know what happened now. But at the time, when I couldn't find you, and you weren't at the LARP party, I figured you were just out to have some fun. You know, no strings attached."

"Not our Petir," said his grandfather. "Please, what means, 'rune'?"

"It's like a magical mark. Or a symbol," said Rianne.

"What magic?" asked his grandmother.

"I just know what the Gypsy said," answered Rianne. "If it be the anniversary of your birth when you first kiss, that blessed moment over the ancient rune becomes your union of destiny."

"Forgive, please, but what does *that* mean?" asked *Abuela*.

"That's what I said," said Petir. "Basically, it means if you get kissed on your birthday over the rune, it's true love."

"You kissed me for the first time on your birthday, over the rune pendant hanging from my neck. Do you think we are destined?"

"Well, let's approach this scientifically," Petir teased. "Do you have any evidence the rune works?"

Surprise crossed her face. "As a matter of fact, I do. Uncle Arthur kissed Aunt Gwen on her birthday on that very same kissing booth."

"*Fíjate,* Gypsy Ana, she do this for a long time," laughed *Abuelo*.

"*Sí.* Of course you destined," said *Abuela*. "Robin Hood, he always get the girl."

"Robin Hood? You are confusing me, *Abuela*. If anyone is supposed to be Robin Hood in this story, it would be Rianne. She's the archer."

"No, no, *mi hijo*. You mother, God rest her, she love Robin Hood story, so she name you Robin Hood."

"Noooo. She named me Petir."

"*Si, Petirrojo*. It mean 'robin' *en español*.You know, robin."
Petir's *abuelo* began whistling and flapping his arms.

"You mean like the bird? The robin redbreast?" said Rianne.

"*Si, si. Rojo* is red."

"*Capota*, it mean hood," nodded *Abuela*. "*Petirrojo Capota*'
is Robin Hood." She smiled triumphantly.

"Seriously? And no one thought to mention that?" said Petir.

"Robin Hood find Maid Rianne. Is very close. Like the
story," added *Abuela*.

"Actually, my given name is Marianne."

"Seriously? How do you get Rianne out of Marion?" asked
Petir.

"It's M-A-R-I-A-N-N-E. When I lost my parents, I was little,
and my folks shortened it to Rianne." She shrugged. "You know,
new home, new family, new life…new name. They were trying to
make things easier."

"Robin Hood and Maid Marianne. It is destiny for me," said
*Abuela*. "Stand for picture. Your parents smile down on you both
today. You beautiful girl and beautiful boy."

Petir looked at Rianne. Most likely, he was sporting what
Chris had dubbed his "goofy look," but he didn't care. After two
months, Petir still couldn't believe his good fortune. Rianne was
both sexy and demur in her little black dress and string of pearls,
perfectly matching his white shirt and black suit. Amazing how
she could rock a cocktail dress and heels the same way she rocked
old-time gowns.

"Yup, it's settled. Maid Marianne belongs with Robin
Hood." Petir held her close for the camera. Rianne wrapped her
arms around his waist and smiled up at him.

Mystical rune?

Storybook destiny?

Whatever.

This was living the dream.


The End?

## The Legend

*If it be the anniversary of your birth when you first kiss, that blessed moment over the ancient rune becomes your union of destiny.*

Long ago, before time had forgotten, an ordinary tree was forever changed when a magical rune was carved into its trunk. To keep its power out of the hands of those who would abuse it, the tree was taken down and cut into boards. Although the boards were used to construct a Gypsy's mystical Kissing Booth, many said the destruction of the tree was the undoing of its magical power.

What do you believe?
Read the tales of the *Love of Fairs* series, and decide for yourself.

www.DeborahAnnDavis.com

# FACTOIDS & GLOSSARY

## Random Factoids

*Assassin's Creed* – electronic game by X-Box

**Bears in Simsbury, CT** – Yes, we have bears in Connecticut
http://www.depdata.ct.gov/wildlife/sighting/bearsight.asp

**Phillip Fagans** – woodcarver from 1930s who said there were
two types of carvers; those who carve to aid their thought, and
those who thought to aid their carving."

**Amsterdam Maid (A-Rovin') – to hear the traditional sea
shanty: http://chivalry.com/cantaria/lyrics/amstmaid.html**

## Spanish for Beginners

*Abuela* – Grandmother      *Abuelo* – Grandfather

*Boricuas* – Natives of Puerto Rico who often call their island
      *Borinquen*

*Capota* – Hood

*En español* – In Spanish

*Fíjate* – Imagine that!

*Mi hijo* – My son/child; term of endearment

*Petirrojo* – Robin Redbreast, song bird

*Por supuesto* – of course

## <u>Vocabulary for Anyone</u>

**British Soldiers** – red topped lichen used for red-pink dye

**Fiddleheads** – early form of ferns before they unfurl. Edible once the outer coating is removed.

**Geodashing** – a race that interfaces the internet with real life. A computer randomly generates dashpoints from all over the world, and competitors (individual or team) try to physically reach as many as they can within the time limit http://gpstracklog.com/2007/01/geodashing_and_.html

**GPS** – Global Positioning System

**LARP** – Live Action Role Playing

**Milkweed** – any one of several plants that secrete a milky substance with edible young shoots

**Porridge**- Oatmeal

**Quarterstaff** – a stout pole, 6-8 feet long, used as a weapon

**Rune** – a mark or letter of mysterious or magic significance

**Staff** – a stout stick used as a weapon

**Treacle** – a blend of molasses, sugar, and corn syrup

**UConn** – University of Connecticut

**Venison** – deer meat

**X-Box** – a very popular video game console

**SNEAK A PEEK:**

**LOVE of FAIRS Series**
Different Time Periods…Different Characters…Same
Legend…

I hope you enjoyed reading *Fairly Certain*, the first tale in
the **Love of Fairs series,** as much as I enjoyed writing it.

Here is an excerpt from *Fairly Safe*, the second tale in the
**Love of Fairs series.** Sign up for notification when it launches
autumn 2014 at <u>pre@DeborahAnnDavis.com</u>.

\*\*\*

Heart pounding, Jacob
Kent stepped out of his car as
he scanned the fair on the far
side of the parking lot. What if
he had misinterpreted the clues
and was at the wrong place?

As with many country
fairs, the parking lot was no
more than an abused pasture.
This one was almost the size of
two football fields. Fair
employees decked in bright
yellow directed the early trickle
of cars to their temporary
berths. Jacob ignored them,
choosing instead a parking spot near the exit. Anticipating the
possible need for a quick getaway outweighed a pimply teen's
futile attempts to redirect him.

He regarded the rides twirling and spinning above and around the strolling families. Despite the morning sun, the lights flashed merrily, beckoning to all. At 10 a.m. it wasn't crowded, but he knew that would soon change. Locking his car, he slowly picked his way through the beaten grass, combing all directions for a clue the girls were there. As the unmistakable sound of carnival music floated toward him on the warm summer breeze, he reviewed his plan

First, he would walk through the fair to familiarize himself with the layout they had printed out. Then he would adjust their escape route to where he parked the car. After assessing the grounds, he would plant himself somewhere along the concourse, and watch the crowd. That's how he had always found Casey in the past, and that's how he was going to find her again.

A voice came over the loudspeaker, momentarily dimming the carnival noise. "Would the owner of a red ford pickup truck, license plate DAG537, please return to your vehicle? Your lights are on."

Jacob tensed. Was that some kind of clue? He looked over the parking lot. No, he could see the lights of the red truck from here. He smiled ruefully to himself.

*Get a grip, Kent,* he thought as he watched a portly balding man march exasperatedly toward the truck

He sighed. Intellectually, he had to acknowledge they might have pieced together a bunch of randomly forgotten items into a fantastical story, but emotionally, he couldn't help but believe the items served an ultimate purpose. If The Herd was here, he was going to find them. He also knew if he wasn't careful, he could spend the entire day jumping at shadows and following dead ends

*Like that little commotion over by the edge of the fair.* To his over-active imagination, that game of tag could look like a child trying to escape from the evil clutches of—

"HAHAHAHAHAHAHA, WIPEOUT!" sang out over the loudspeaker.

His head jerked up. As the pounding drums from the familiar song drowned out the carnival music, all doubt was erased. The loudspeaker was sending out a warning. His eyes darted back toward the commotion he had noticed. That was no game of tag. That was a child trying to escape a man in hot pursuit. Jacob couldn't be positive at this distance, but it sure looked like Robin. With his heart in his throat, he broke into a run, zigzagging between cars, trying to intercept the fleeing child as it headed toward the side of the parking lot. In this surreal moment, the same song they had used for obstacle course training was being piped out like background music to a scene in a movie. But this scene was real, where a real menace was gaining. Caught in his own nightmare, Jacob was watching Robin run for her life, and he was not close enough to help.

As the predator and prey crossed the area between the fair and the parking lot, the longer legs of the adult closed the gap between them, but once they reached the cars, the advantage became hers. Robin's small size and training put some distance between them as she dodged around vehicles. However, her constant change of direction made it difficult for Jacob to maintain a course of interception. Watching Robin's progress, Jacob realized she was trying to head back toward the fair. Silently applauding Robin's decision to get closer to other people who could help her, Jacob altered his course accordingly.

So did Robin's pursuer.

Suddenly, her stalker eliminated the space between them by clambering up and over two pickup trucks, and landing an arm's length away. Skidding, Robin veered around another vehicle with the man on her tail. As Jacob frantically tried to reach her, a brunette Sam suddenly popped out from behind a car and neatly took the man out with one magnificent sweep of a skateboard to the head.

*Where did she come from?* A stunned Jacob skidded to a stop, gasping for breath, his chest burning.

With a quick high-five, the sisters raced back to the fair. Jacob tried in vain to get their attention, but he hadn't quite recovered enough breath to formulate sounds louder than gasps. He shook his head as he tried to calm the burning in his lungs. He was a wreck, but they were able to *run* off.

*And I was going to save them?* He weakly chuckled. *What was I thinking?*

Sobering, he trotted over to the man who was staggering to his feet. With rage marshalling all of his strength, Jacob drew back and smashed his fist into the man's face. The unexpected pain in his fist was nothing compared to the satisfaction of watching Robin's former threat drop like an anchor.

Shaking the pain out of his hand, Jacob aimed a vindictive kick at the ribs of his girls' attacker. Any qualms he might ordinarily have about hitting a man when he's down were nonexistent when it came to someone threatening his girls. Satisfied the man was no longer a danger, he took off in the direction he had seen the girls disappear, trying to calm the fear rising in his chest. He doubted this man had come alone. The girls probably knew that, too, and would be hiding. How was he going to find them before their pursuers did?

The light glinting off the speaker perched atop a telephone pole caught his eye. Jacob skidded to a stop and stared at it.

*Of course* When Robin had been trying to escape, that speaker had been blasting out *Wipe Out!,* but now he only heard carnival music. With a grin, Jacob decided it was time to stop believing in coincidences. Someone at the fair must be helping them. If he found that person, he'd be able to find the fugitives

\*\*\*

If you enjoyed this excerpt from ***Fairly Safe***, the second tale in the **Love of Fairs series,** sign up for notification when it launches in Autumn 2014 at pre@DeborahAnnDavis.com. I look forward to your feedback.

Make it a fabulous day!

DEBORAH ANN DAVIS has enthusiastically taught Science (Biology, Earth Sciences, Environmental Science) for 25+ years. She is also an Educational Speaker and a Certified Personal Trainer.

Even though they had followed separate paths, Deborah reunited with, and married her childhood sweetheart, twelve years after their first kiss. Somewhere in the middle of all that educating, she stepped out of teaching for 6 years to do the Mommy Thing, and run the office for their family construction company. During that time, she and her husband coached their daughter's AAU Basketball Team, which swept States two years in a row. (Yay!) For several years their daughter and their money went to college.

Deborah currently resides on a lovely lake in Connecticut with her husband. She enjoys dabbling with living a sustainable life, writing novels for her Love of Fairs series, dancing, playing outside, and laughing really hard every day. She promotes increasing the amount of movement throughout your day via Wiggle Writer posts on Merry Meddling, her blog at www.DeborahAnnDavis.com. Follow her @DeborahAnnDavis.

*"Variety is the spice of life."*
— **Someone Really Smart**

*"If Variety is the spice of life, Humor is my favorite flavor."*
**–Deborah Ann Davis**